Timeless Love

POEMS, STORIES, and LETTERS

T0282252

All content is in the public domain.

Editor's note: In order to preserve the authenticity of these works, many old, variant spellings (and misspellings) of words have been maintained. We have made only minor adjustments to punctuation uses in order to improve readability.

ISBN 978-1-4003-4184-9 (TP)
ISBN 978-0-7852-4841-5 (downloadable audio)

Library of Congress Cataloging-in-Publication Data

Names: Bailey, Jocelyn L., editor.
Title: Timeless love : poems, stories, and letters / [edited by
    Jocelyn Bailey].
Description: [Nashville] : [Thomas Nelson], [2020] | Summary:
    "This beautiful, giftable collection celebrates the beauty and
    the agony of love through classic poems, stories, and letters
    from beloved writers"-- Provided by publisher.
Identifiers: LCCN 2020027073 | ISBN 9780785245919
    (hardcover) | ISBN 9780785246244 (epub) | ISBN
    9780785248415
Subjects: LCSH: Love--Literary collections.
Classification: LCC PN6071.L7 T56 2020 | DDC
    808.8/03543--dc23
LC record available at https://lccn.loc.gov/2020027073

Printed in the United States of America

23 24 25 26 27 **LBC** 5 4 3 2 1

Contents

POEMS

iii

CONTENTS

CONTENTS

STORIES

LETTERS

Poems

William Shakespeare

1564–1616

Sonnet 18

Shall I compare thee to a summer's day?
Thou art more lovely and more temperate.
Rough winds do shake the darling buds of May,
And summer's lease hath all too short a date.
Sometime too hot the eye of heaven shines,
And often is his gold complexion dimm'd;
And every fair from fair sometime declines,
By chance, or nature's changing course,
    untrimm'd;
But thy eternal summer shall not fade,
Nor lose possession of that fair thou ow'st,

Nor shall death brag thou wander'st in his shade,

When in eternal lines to Time thou grow'st.

      So long as men can breathe, or eyes

          can see,

      So long lives this, and this gives life

          to thee.

Sonnet 55

Not marble nor the gilded monuments
Of princes shall outlive this powerful rhyme;
But you shall shine more bright in these contents
Than unswept stone, besmear'd with
    sluttish time.
When wasteful war shall statues overturn,
And broils root out the work of masonry,
Nor Mars his sword nor war's quick fire shall
    burn
The living record of your memory.
'Gainst death and all-oblivious enmity

7

Shall you pace forth; your praise shall still
    find room,
Even in the eyes of all posterity
That wear this world out to the ending doom.
        So, till the Judgement that yourself
          arise,
          You live in this, and dwell in lovers'
          eyes.

Sonnet 130

My mistress' eyes are nothing like the sun;
Coral is far more red than her lips' red;
If snow be white, why then her breasts are dun;
If hairs be wires, black wires grow on her head.
I have seen roses damasked, red and white,
But no such roses see I in her cheeks;
And in some perfumes is there more delight
Than in the breath that from my mistress reeks.
I love to hear her speak, yet well I know
That music hath a far more pleasing sound;
I grant I never saw a goddess go;

My mistress when she walks treads on the
    ground.
        And yet, by heaven, I think my love as
          rare
        As any she belied with false compare.

Sonnet 147

My love is as a fever, longing still

For that which longer nurseth the disease;

Feeding on that which doth preserve the sill,

The uncertain sickly appetite to please.

My reason, the physician to my love,

Angry that his prescriptions are not kept,

Hath left me, and I desperate now approve

Desire is death, which physic did except.

Past cure I am, now reason is past care,

And frantic-mad with evermore unrest;

My thoughts and my discourse as madmen's are,

At random from the truth vainly express'd;
>   For I have sworn thee fair and thought
>   thee bright,
>   Who art as black as hell, as dark as
>   night.

John Keats

1795–1821

To Fanny

Physician Nature! let my spirit blood!
    O ease my heart of verse and let
      me rest;
Throw me upon thy tripod, till the flood
    Of stifling numbers ebbs from my full
      breast.
A theme! a theme! Great Nature! give a theme;
      Let me begin my dream.
I come—I see thee, as thou standest there,
Beckon me out into the wintry air.

Ah! dearest love, sweet home of all my fears
And hopes and joys and panting
miseries,—
To-night, if I may guess, thy beauty wears
A smile of such delight,
As brilliant and as bright,
As when with ravished, aching,
vassal eyes,
Lost in a soft amaze,
I gaze, I gaze!

Who now, with greedy looks, eats up my feast?
What stare outfaces now my
silver moon!
Ah! keep that hand unravished at the least;
Let, let the amorous burn—
But, prithee, do not turn
The current of your heart from me
so soon:
O save, in charity,
The quickest pulse for me.

Save it for me, sweet love! though music breathe
        Voluptuous visions into the warm air,
Though swimming through the dance's
    dangerous wreath,
          Be like an April day,
          Smiling and cold and gay,
     A temperate lily, temperate as fair;
          Then, heaven! there will be
          A warmer June for me.

Why this, you'll say—my Fanny!—is not true;
        Put your soft hand upon your
    snowy side,
Where the heart beats: confess—'tis
    nothing new—
          Must not a woman be
          A feather on the sea,
     Swayed to and fro by every wind
     and tide?
          Of as uncertain speed
          As blow-ball from the mead?

I know it—and to know it is despair
　　　To one who loves you as I love, sweet
　　　Fanny,
Whose heart goes fluttering for you every where,
　　　Nor when away you roam,
　　　Dare keep its wretched home:
Love, love alone, has pains severe
　　　and many;
　　　Then, loveliest! keep me free
　　　From torturing jealousy.

Ah! if you prize my subdued soul above
　　　The poor, the fading, brief pride of
　　　an hour:
Let none profane my Holy See of Love,
　　　Or with a rude hand break
　　　The sacramental cake:
Let none else touch the just new-
　　　budded flower;
　　　If not—may my eyes close,
　　　Love, on their last repose!

Bright Star

Bright star! would I were steadfast as thou art—
      Not in lone splendour hung aloft the
          night,
And watching, with eternal lids apart,
      Like Nature's patient sleepless Eremite,
The moving waters at their priestlike task
      Of pure ablution round earth's human
          shores,
Or gazing on the new soft fallen mask
      Of snow upon the mountains and the
          moors—

No—yet still steadfast, still unchangeable,
      Pillow'd upon my fair love's ripening
         breast,
To feel for ever its soft fall and swell,
      Awake for ever in a sweet unrest,
Still, still to hear her tender-taken breath,
And so live ever—or else swoon to death.

Elizabeth Barrett Browning

1806–1861

Yet, Love, Mere Love, Is Beautiful Indeed

(Sonnet 10)

Yet, love, mere love, is beautiful indeed
And worthy of acceptation. Fire is bright,
Let temple burn, or flax; an equal light
Leaps in the flame from cedar-plank or weed:
And love is fire. And when I say at need
I love thee—mark!—*I love thee*—in thy sight

I stand transfigured, glorified aright,
With conscience of the new rays that proceed
Out of my face toward thine. There's nothing low
In love, when love the lowest: meanest creatures
Who love God, God accepts while loving so.
And what I *feel*, across the inferior features
Of what I *am*, doth flash itself, and show
How that great work of Love enhances Nature's.

If Thou Must Love Me

(Sonnet 14)

If thou must love me, let it be for nought
Except for love's sake only. Do not say,
"I love her for her smile—her look—her way
Of speaking gently,—for a trick of thought
That falls in well with mine, and certes brought
A sense of pleasant ease on such a day"—
For these things in themselves, Belovèd, may

Be changed, or change for thee—and love, so
    wrought,
May be unwrought so. Neither love me for
Thine own dear pity's wiping my cheeks dry:
A creature might forget to weep, who bore
Thy comfort long, and lose thy love thereby!
But love me for love's sake, that evermore
Thou may'st love on, through love's eternity.

How Do I Love Thee?

(Sonnet 43)

How do I love thee? Let me count the ways.
I love thee to the depth and breadth and height
My soul can reach, when feeling out of sight
For the ends of being and ideal grace.
I love thee to the level of every day's
Most quiet need, by sun and candle-light.
I love thee freely, as men strive for right.
I love thee purely, as they turn from praise.

I love thee with the passion put to use
In my old griefs, and with my childhood's faith.
I love thee with a love I seemed to lose
With my lost saints. I love thee with the breath,
Smiles, tears, of all my life; and, if God choose,
I shall but love thee better after death.

William Wordsworth

1770–1850

Perfect Woman

She was a phantom of delight
When first she gleam'd upon my sight;
A lovely apparition, sent
To be a moment's ornament;
Her eyes as stars of twilight fair;
Like twilight's, too, her dusky hair;
But all things else about her drawn
From May-time and the cheerful dawn;
A dancing shape, an image gay,
To haunt, to startle, and waylay.

      I saw her upon nearer view,

A Spirit, yet a Woman too!
Her household motions light and free,
And steps of virgin liberty;
A countenance in which did meet
Sweet records, promises as sweet;
A creature not too bright or good
For human nature's daily food;
For transient sorrows, simple wiles,
Praise, blame, love, kisses, tears, and
    smiles.
And now I see with eye serene
The very pulse of the machine;
A being breathing thoughtful breath,
A traveller between life and death;
The reason firm, the temperate will,
Endurance, foresight, strength, and
    skill;
A perfect Woman, nobly plann'd,
To warn, to comfort, and command;
And yet a Spirit still, and bright
With something of angelic light.

Robert Burns

1759–1796

A Red, Red Rose

O my luve's like a red, red rose,
That's newly sprung in June;
O my luve's like the melodie
That's sweetly played in tune.
As fair art thou, my bonnie lass,
So deep in luve am I;
And I will luve thee still, my dear,
Till a' the seas gang dry.
Till a' the seas gang dry, my dear,
And the rocks melt wi' the sun:
O I will love thee still, my dear,

While the sands o' life shall run.
And fare thee weel, my only luve,
And fare thee weel awhile!
And I will come again, my luve,
Though it were ten thousand mile.

Anna, Thy Charms

Anna, thy charms my bosom fire,
      And waste my soul with care;
But ah! how bootless to admire,
      When fated to despair!

Yet in thy presence, lovely Fair,
      To hope may be forgiven;
For sure 'twere impious to despair
      So much in sight of heaven.

Christina Rossetti

1830–1894

Monna Innominata
[I loved you first]

I loved you first: but afterwards your love,
Outsoaring mine, sang such a loftier song
As drowned the friendly cooings of my dove.
Which owes the other most? my love was long,
And yours one moment seemed to wax more
      strong;
I loved and guessed at you, you construed me
And loved me for what might or might not be—
Nay, weights and measures do us both a wrong.

For verily love knows not 'mine' or 'thine';
With separate 'I' and 'thou' free love has done,
For one is both and both are one in love:
Rich love knows nought of 'thine that is
      not mine';
Both have the strength and both the length
      thereof,
Both of us, of the love which makes us one.

A Birthday

My heart is like a singing bird
    Whose nest is in a water'd shoot;
My heart is like an apple-tree
    Whose boughs are bent with thick-set
      fruit;
My heart is like a rainbow shell
    That paddles in a halcyon sea;
My heart is gladder than all these,
    Because my love is come to me.

Raise me a daïs of silk and down;
      Hang it with vair and purple dyes;
Carve it in doves and pomegranates,
      And peacocks with a hundred eyes;
Work it in gold and silver grapes,
      In leaves and silver fleurs-de-lys;
Because the birthday of my life
      Is come, my love is come to me.

Mary Weston Fordham

1842–1904

For Who?

When the heavens with stars are gleaming
      Like a diadem of light,
And the moon's pale rays are streaming,
      Decking earth with radiance bright;
When the autumn's winds are sighing,
      O'er the hill and o'er the lea,
When the summer time is dying,
      Wanderer, wilt thou think of me?

When thy life is crowned with gladness,
        And thy home with love is blest,
Not one brow o'ercast with sadness,
        Not one bosom of unrest—
When at eventide reclining,
        At thy hearthstone gay and free,
Think of one whose life is pining,
        Breathe thou, love, a prayer for me.

Should dark sorrows make thee languish,
        Cause thy cheek to lose its hue,
In the hour of deepest anguish,
        Darling, then I'll grieve with you.
Though the night be dark and dreary,
        And it seemeth long to thee,
I would whisper, "be not weary;"
        I would pray love, then, for thee.

Well I know that in the future,
        I may cherish naught of earth;
Well I know that love needs nurture,
        And it is of heavenly birth.

FOR WHO?

But though ocean waves may sever
      I from thee, and thee from me,
Still this constant heart will never,
      Never cease to think of thee.

Paul Laurence Dunbar

1872–1906

Invitation to Love

Come when the nights are bright with stars
  Or when the moon is mellow;
Come when the sun his golden bars
  Drops on the hay-field yellow.
Come in the twilight soft and gray,
Come in the night or come in the day,
Come, O love, whene'er you may,
  And you are welcome, welcome.

You are sweet, O Love, dear Love,
You are soft as the nesting dove.
Come to my heart and bring it rest
As the bird flies home to its welcome nest.

Come when my heart is full of grief
            Or when my heart is merry;
Come with the falling of the leaf
            Or with the redd'ning cherry.
Come when the year's first blossom blows,
Come when the summer gleams and glows,
Come with the winter's drifting snows,
            And you are welcome, welcome.

Alice Dunbar-Nelson

1875–1935

Farewell

Farewell, sweetheart, and again farewell;
To day we part, and who can tell
      If we shall e'er again
Meet, and with clasped hands
Renew our vows of love, and forget
      The sad, dull pain.
Dear heart, 'tis bitter thus to lose thee
And think mayhap, you will forget me;
      And yet, I thrill
As I remember long and happy days

Fraught with sweet love and pleasant memories
       That linger still
You go to loved ones who will smile
And clasp you in their arms, and all the while
       I stay and moan
For you, my love, my heart and strive
To gather up life's dull, gray thread
       And walk alone.
Aye, with you love the red and gold
Goes from my life, and leaves it cold
       And dull and bare,
Why should I strive to live and learn
And smile and jest, and daily try
       You from my heart to tare?
Nay, sweetheart, rather would I lie
Me down, and sleep for aye; or fly
       To regions far
Where cruel Fate is not and lovers live
Nor feel the grim, cold hand of Destiny
       Their way to bar.
I murmur not, dear love, I only say

Again farewell. God bless the day
       On which we met,
And bless you too, my love, and be with you
In sorrow or in happiness, nor let you
       E'er me forget.

Stories

Oscar Wilde

1854–1900

The Nightingale and the Rose

"S he said that she would dance with me if I brought her red roses," cried the young Student; "but in all my garden there is no red rose."

From her nest in the holm-oak tree the Nightingale heard him, and she looked out through the leaves, and wondered.

"No red rose in all my garden!" he cried, and his beautiful eyes filled with tears. "Ah, on what little things does happiness depend! I have read all that the wise men have written, and all the secrets of philosophy are mine, yet for want of a red rose is my life made wretched."

"Here at last is a true lover," said the Nightingale. "Night after night have I sung of him, though I knew him not: night after night have I told his story to the stars, and now I see him. His hair is dark as the hyacinth-blossom, and his lips are red as the rose of his desire; but passion has made his face like pale ivory, and sorrow has set her seal upon his brow."

"The Prince gives a ball to-morrow night," murmured the young Student, "and my love will be of the company. If I bring her a red rose she will dance with me till dawn. If I bring her a red rose, I shall hold her in my arms, and she will lean her head upon my shoulder, and her hand will be clasped in mine. But there is no red rose in my garden, so I shall sit lonely, and she will pass me by. She will have no heed of me, and my heart will break."

"Here indeed is the true lover," said the Nightingale. "What I sing of, he suffers—what is joy to me, to him is pain. Surely Love is a wonderful thing. It is more precious than emeralds, and dearer than fine opals. Pearls and pomegranates cannot buy it, nor is it set forth in the marketplace. It may not be purchased of the merchants, nor can it be weighed out in the balance for gold."

"The musicians will sit in their gallery," said the young Student, "and play upon their stringed instruments, and my love will dance to the sound of the harp and the violin. She will dance so lightly that her feet will not touch the floor, and the courtiers in their gay dresses will throng round her. But with me she will not dance, for I have no red rose to give her"; and he flung himself down on the grass, and buried his face in his hands, and wept.

"Why is he weeping?" asked a little Green Lizard, as he ran past him with his tail in the air.

"Why, indeed?" said a Butterfly, who was fluttering about after a sunbeam.

"Why, indeed?" whispered a Daisy to his neighbour, in a soft, low voice.

"He is weeping for a red rose," said the Nightingale.

"For a red rose?" they cried; "how very ridiculous!" and the little Lizard, who was something of a cynic, laughed outright.

But the Nightingale understood the secret of the Student's sorrow, and she sat silent in the oak-tree, and thought about the mystery of Love.

Suddenly she spread her brown wings for flight, and soared into the air. She passed through the grove like a shadow, and like a shadow she sailed across the garden.

In the centre of the grass-plot was standing a beautiful Rose-tree, and when she saw it she flew over to it, and lit upon a spray.

"Give me a red rose," she cried, "and I will sing you my sweetest song."

But the Tree shook its head.

"My roses are white," it answered; "as white as the foam of the sea, and whiter than the snow upon the mountain. But go to my brother who grows round the old sun-dial, and perhaps he will give you what you want."

So the Nightingale flew over to the Rose-tree that was growing round the old sun-dial.

"Give me a red rose," she cried, "and I will sing you my sweetest song."

But the Tree shook its head.

"My roses are yellow," it answered; "as yellow as

the hair of the mermaiden who sits upon an amber throne, and yellower than the daffodil that blooms in the meadow before the mower comes with his scythe. But go to my brother who grows beneath the Student's window, and perhaps he will give you what you want."

So the Nightingale flew over to the Rose-tree that was growing beneath the Student's window.

"Give me a red rose," she cried, "and I will sing you my sweetest song."

But the Tree shook its head.

"My roses are red," it answered, "as red as the feet of the dove, and redder than the great fans of coral that wave and wave in the ocean-cavern. But the winter has chilled my veins, and the frost has nipped my buds, and the storm has broken my branches, and I shall have no roses at all this year."

"One red rose is all I want," cried the Nightingale, "only one red rose! Is there no way by which I can get it?"

"There is a way," answered the Tree; "but it is so terrible that I dare not tell it to you."

"Tell it to me," said the Nightingale, "I am not afraid."

"If you want a red rose," said the Tree, "you must build it out of music by moonlight, and stain it with your own heart's-blood. You must sing to me with your breast against a thorn. All night long you must sing to me, and the thorn must pierce your heart, and your life-blood must flow into my veins, and become mine."

"Death is a great price to pay for a red rose," cried the Nightingale, "and Life is very dear to all. It is pleasant to sit in the green wood, and to watch the Sun in his chariot of gold, and the Moon in her chariot of pearl. Sweet is the scent of the hawthorn, and sweet are the bluebells that hide in the valley, and the heather that blows on the hill. Yet Love is better than Life, and what is the heart of a bird compared to the heart of a man?"

So she spread her brown wings for flight, and soared into the air. She swept over the garden like a shadow, and like a shadow she sailed through the grove.

The young Student was still lying on the grass, where she had left him, and the tears were not yet dry in his beautiful eyes.

"Be happy," cried the Nightingale, "be happy; you shall have your red rose. I will build it out of music by moonlight, and stain it with my own heart's-blood. All that I ask of you in return is that you will be a true lover, for Love is wiser than Philosophy, though she is wise, and mightier than Power, though he is mighty. Flame-coloured are his wings, and coloured like flame is his body. His lips are sweet as honey, and his breath is like frankincense."

The Student looked up from the grass, and listened, but he could not understand what the Nightingale was saying to him, for he only knew the things that are written down in books.

But the Oak-tree understood, and felt sad, for he was very fond of the little Nightingale who had built her nest in his branches.

"Sing me one last song," he whispered; "I shall feel very lonely when you are gone."

So the Nightingale sang to the Oak-tree, and her voice was like water bubbling from a silver jar.

When she had finished her song the Student got up, and pulled a note-book and a lead-pencil out of his pocket.

"She has form," he said to himself, as he walked

away through the grove—"That cannot be denied to her; but has she got feeling? I am afraid not. In fact, she is like most artists; she is all style, without any sincerity. She would not sacrifice herself for others. She thinks merely of music, and everybody knows that the arts are selfish. Still, it must be admitted that she has some beautiful notes in her voice. What a pity it is that they do not mean anything, or do any practical good." And he went into his room, and lay down on his little pallet-bed, and began to think of his love; and, after a time, he fell asleep.

And when the Moon shone in the heavens the Nightingale flew to the Rose-tree, and set her breast against the thorn. All night long she sang with her breast against the thorn, and the cold crystal Moon leaned down and listened. All night long she sang, and the thorn went deeper and deeper into her breast, and her life-blood ebbed away from her.

She sang first of the birth of love in the heart of a boy and a girl. And on the top-most spray of the Rose-tree there blossomed a marvellous rose, petal following petal, as song followed song. Pale was it, at first, as the mist that hangs over the river—pale as the feet of the morning, and silver as the wings of the dawn. As the shadow of a rose in a mirror of silver, as the shadow of a rose in a water-pool, so was the rose that blossomed on the topmost spray of the Tree.

But the Tree cried to the Nightingale to press closer against the thorn. "Press closer, little Nightingale," cried the Tree, "or the Day will come before the rose is finished."

So the Nightingale pressed closer against the thorn, and louder and louder grew her song, for she sang of the birth of passion in the soul of a man and a maid.

And a delicate flush of pink came into the leaves of the rose, like the flush in the face of the bridegroom when he kisses the lips of the bride. But the thorn had not yet reached her heart, so the rose's heart remained white, for only a Nightingale's heart's-blood can crimson the heart of a rose.

And the Tree cried to the Nightingale to press closer against the thorn. "Press closer, little Nightingale," cried the Tree, "or the Day will come before the rose is finished."

So the Nightingale pressed closer against the thorn, and the thorn touched her heart, and a fierce pang of pain shot through her. Bitter, bitter was the pain, and wilder and wilder grew her song, for she sang of the Love that is perfected by Death, of the Love that dies not in the tomb.

And the marvellous rose became crimson, like the rose of the eastern sky. Crimson was the girdle of petals, and crimson as a ruby was the heart.

But the Nightingale's voice grew fainter, and her little wings began to beat, and a film came over her eyes. Fainter and fainter grew her song, and she felt something choking her in her throat.

Then she gave one last burst of music. The white Moon heard it, and she forgot the dawn, and lingered on in the sky. The red rose heard it, and it trembled all over with ecstasy, and opened its petals to the cold morning air. Echo bore it to her purple cavern in the hills, and woke the sleeping shepherds from their dreams. It floated through the reeds of the river, and they carried its message to the sea.

"Look, look!" cried the Tree, "the rose is finished

now"; but the Nightingale made no answer, for she was lying dead in the long grass, with the thorn in her heart.

And at noon the Student opened his window and looked out.

"Why, what a wonderful piece of luck!" he cried; "here is a red rose! I have never seen any rose like it in all my life. It is so beautiful that I am sure it has a long Latin name"; and he leaned down and plucked it.

Then he put on his hat, and ran up to the Professor's house with the rose in his hand.

The daughter of the Professor was sitting in the doorway winding blue silk on a reel, and her little dog was lying at her feet.

"You said that you would dance with me if I brought you a red rose," cried the Student. "Here is the reddest rose in all the world. You will wear it to-night next your heart, and as we dance together it will tell you how I love you."

But the girl frowned.

"I am afraid it will not go with my dress," she answered; "and, besides, the Chamberlain's nephew has sent me some real jewels, and everybody knows that jewels cost far more than flowers."

"Well, upon my word, you are very ungrateful," said the Student angrily; and he threw the rose into the street, where it fell into the gutter, and a cart-wheel went over it.

"Ungrateful!" said the girl. "I tell you what, you are very rude; and, after all, who are you? Only a Student. Why, I don't believe you have even got silver buckles to your shoes as the Chamberlain's nephew has"; and she got up from her chair and went into the house.

"What a silly thing Love is," said the Student as he walked away. "It is not half as useful as Logic, for it does not prove anything, and it is always telling one of things that are not going to happen, and making one believe things that are not true. In fact, it is quite unpractical, and, as in this age to be practical is everything, I shall go back to Philosophy and study Metaphysics."

So he returned to his room and pulled out a great dusty book, and began to read.

Edith Wharton

1862–1937

The Fulness of Life

I

For hours she had lain in a kind of gentle torpor, not unlike that sweet lassitude which masters one in the hush of a midsummer noon, when the heat seems to have silenced the very birds and insects, and, lying sunk in the tasselled meadow-grasses, one looks up through a level roofing of maple-leaves at the vast shadowless, and unsuggestive blue. Now and then, at ever-lengthening intervals, a flash of pain darted through her, like the ripple of sheet-lightning across such a midsummer sky; but it was too transitory to shake her stupor, that calm, delicious, bottomless stupor into which she felt herself sinking more and more deeply, without a disturbing impulse of resistance, an effort of reattachment to the vanishing edges of consciousness.

The resistance, the effort, had known their hour of violence; but now they were at an end. Through her mind, long harried by grotesque visions, fragmentary images of the life that she was leaving, tormenting lines of verse, obstinate presentments of pictures once beheld, indistinct impressions of rivers, towers, and cupolas, gathered in the length of journeys half forgotten—through her mind there now only moved a few primal sensations of colorless well-being; a vague satisfaction in the thought that she had swallowed her noxious last draught of medicine . . . and that she should never again hear the creaking of her husband's boots—those horrible boots—and that no one would come to bother her about the next day's dinner . . . or the butcher's book . . .

At last even these dim sensations spent themselves

in the thickening obscurity which enveloped her; a dusk now filled with pale geometric roses, circling softly, interminably before her, now darkened to a uniform blue-blackness, the hue of a summer night without stars. And into this darkness she felt herself sinking, sinking, with the gentle sense of security of one upheld from beneath. Like a tepid tide it rose around her, gliding ever higher and higher, folding in its velvety embrace her relaxed and tired body, now submerging her breast and shoulders, now creeping gradually, with soft inexorableness, over her throat to her chin, to her ears, to her mouth. . . . Ah, now it was rising too high; the impulse to struggle was renewed . . . her mouth was full . . . she was choking. . . . Help!

"It is all over," said the nurse, drawing down the eyelids with official composure.

The clock struck three. They remembered it afterward. Someone opened the window and let in a blast of that strange, neutral air which walks the earth between darkness and dawn; someone else led the husband into another room. He walked vaguely, like a blind man, on his creaking boots.

II

She stood, as it seemed, on a threshold, yet no tangible gateway was in front of her. Only a wide vista of light, mild yet penetrating as the gathered glimmer of innumerable stars, expanded gradually before her eyes, in blissful contrast to the cavernous darkness from which she had of late emerged.

She stepped forward, not frightened, but hesitating, and as her eyes began to grow more familiar with the melting depths of light about her, she distinguished the outlines of a landscape, at first swimming in the opaline uncertainty of Shelley's vaporous creations, then gradually resolved into distincter shape—the vast unrolling of a sunlit plain, aerial forms of mountains, and presently the silver crescent of a river in the valley, and a blue stencilling of trees along its curve— something suggestive in its ineffable hue of an azure background of Leonardo's, strange, enchanting, mysterious, leading on the eye and the imagination into regions of fabulous delight. As she gazed, her heart beat with a soft and rapturous surprise; so exquisite a promise she read in the summons of that hyaline distance.

"And so death is not the end after all," in sheer gladness she heard herself exclaiming aloud. "I always knew that it couldn't be. I believed in Darwin, of course. I do still; but then Darwin himself said that he wasn't sure about the soul—at least, I think he did—and Wallace was a spiritualist; and then there was St. George Mivart—"

Her gaze lost itself in the ethereal remoteness of the mountains.

"How beautiful! How satisfying!" she murmured. "Perhaps now I shall really know what it is to live."

As she spoke she felt a sudden thickening of her heart-beats, and looking up she was aware that before her stood the Spirit of Life.

"Have you never really known what it is to live?" the Spirit of Life asked her.

"I have never known," she replied, "that fulness of life which we all feel ourselves capable of knowing; though my life has not been without scattered hints of it, like the scent of earth which comes to one sometimes far out at sea."

"And what do you call the fulness of life?" the Spirit asked again.

"Oh, I can't tell you, if you don't know," she said, almost reproachfully. "Many words are supposed to define it—love and sympathy are those in commonest use, but I am not even sure that they are the right ones, and so few people really know what they mean."

"You were married," said the Spirit, "yet you did not find the fulness of life in your marriage?"

"Oh, dear, no," she replied, with an indulgent scorn, "my marriage was a very incomplete affair."

"And yet you were fond of your husband?"

"You have hit upon the exact word; I was fond of him, yes, just as I was fond of my grandmother, and the house that I was born in, and my old nurse. Oh, I was fond of him, and we were counted a very happy couple. But I have sometimes thought that a woman's nature is like a great house full of rooms: there is the hall, through which everyone passes in going in and out; the drawing-room, where one receives formal visits; the sitting-room, where the members of the family come and go as they list; but beyond that, far beyond, are other rooms, the handles of whose doors perhaps are never turned; no one knows the way to them, no one knows whither they lead; and in the innermost room, the holy of holies, the soul sits alone and waits for a footstep that never comes."

"And your husband," asked the Spirit, after a pause, "never got beyond the family sitting-room?"

"Never," she returned, impatiently; "and the worst of it was that he was quite content to remain there. He thought it perfectly beautiful, and sometimes, when he was admiring its commonplace furniture, insignificant as the chairs and tables of a hotel parlor, I felt like crying out to him: 'Fool, will you never guess that close at hand are rooms full of treasures and wonders, such as the eye of man hath not seen, rooms that no step has crossed, but that might be yours to live in, could you but find the handle of the door?'"

"Then," the Spirit continued, "those moments of which you lately spoke, which seemed to come to you like scattered hints of the fulness of life, were not shared with your husband?"

"Oh, no—never. He was different. His boots creaked, and he always slammed the door when he went out, and he never read anything but railway novels and the sporting advertisements in the papers—and—and, in short, we never understood each other in the least."

"To what influence, then, did you owe those exquisite sensations?"

"I can hardly tell. Sometimes to the perfume of a flower; sometimes to a verse of Dante or of Shakespeare; sometimes to a picture or a sunset, or to one of those calm days at sea, when one seems to be lying in the hollow of a blue pearl; sometimes, but rarely, to a word spoken by someone who chanced to give utterance, at the right moment, to what I felt but could not express."

"Someone whom you loved?" asked the Spirit.

"I never loved anyone, in that way," she said, rather sadly, "nor was I thinking of any one person when I spoke, but of two or three who, by touching for an instant upon a certain chord of my being, had called forth a single note of that strange melody which seemed sleeping in my soul. It has seldom happened, however, that I have owed such feelings to people; and no one ever gave me a moment of such happiness as it was my lot to feel one evening in the Church of Or San Michele, in Florence."

"Tell me about it," said the Spirit.

"It was near sunset on a rainy spring afternoon in Easter week. The clouds had vanished, dispersed by a sudden wind, and as we entered the church the fiery panes of the high windows shone out like lamps through the dusk. A priest was at the high altar, his white cope a livid spot in the incense-laden obscurity, the light of the candles flickering up and down like fireflies about his head; a few people knelt near by. We stole behind them and sat down on a bench close to the tabernacle of Orcagna.

"Strange to say, though Florence was not new to me, I had never been in the church before; and in that magical light I saw for the first time the inlaid steps, the fluted columns, the sculptured bas-reliefs and canopy of the marvellous shrine. The marble, worn and mellowed by the subtle hand of time, took on an unspeakable rosy hue, suggestive in some remote way of the honey-colored columns of the Parthenon, but more mystic, more complex, a color not born of the sun's inveterate kiss, but made up of cryptal twilight, and the flame of candles upon martyrs' tombs, and gleams of sunset through symbolic panes of chrysoprase and ruby; such a light as illumines the missals in the library of Siena, or burns like a hidden fire through the Madonna of Gian Bellini in the Church of the Redeemer, at Venice; the light of the Middle Ages, richer, more solemn, more significant than the limpid sunshine of Greece.

"The church was silent, but for the wail of the priest and the occasional scraping of a chair against the floor, and as I sat there, bathed in that light, absorbed in rapt contemplation of the marble miracle which rose before me, cunningly wrought as a casket of ivory and enriched with jewel-like incrustations and tarnished gleams of gold, I felt myself borne onward along a mighty current, whose source seemed to be in the very beginning of things, and whose tremendous waters gathered as they went, all the mingled streams of human passion and endeavor. Life in all its varied manifestations of beauty and strangeness seemed weaving a rhythmical dance around me as I moved, and wherever the spirit of man had passed I knew that my foot had once been familiar.

"As I gazed the mediaeval bosses of the tabernacle of Orcagna seemed to melt and flow into their primal forms so that the folded lotus of the Nile and the Greek acanthus were braided with the runic knots and fish-tailed monsters of the North, and all the plastic terror and beauty born of man's hand from the Ganges to the Baltic quivered and mingled in Orcagna's apotheosis of Mary. And so the river bore me on, past the alien face of antique civilizations and the familiar wonders of Greece, till I swam upon the fiercely rushing tide of the Middle Ages, with its swirling eddies of passion, its heaven-reflecting pools of poetry and art; I heard the rhythmic blow of the craftsmen's hammers in the goldsmiths' workshops and on the walls of churches, the party-cries of armed factions in the narrow streets, the organ-roll of Dante's verse, the crackle of the fagots around Arnold of Brescia, the twitter of the swallows to which St. Francis preached, the laughter of the ladies listening on the hill-side to the quips of the Decameron, while plague-struck Florence howled beneath them—all this and much more I heard, joined in strange unison with voices earlier and more remote, fierce, passionate, or tender, yet subdued to such awful harmony that I thought of the song that the morning stars sang together and felt as though it were sounding in my ears. My heart beat to suffocation, the tears burned my lids, the joy, the mystery of it seemed too intolerable to be borne. I could not understand even then the words of the song; but I knew that if there had been someone at my side who could have heard it with me, we might have found the key to it together.

"I turned to my husband, who was sitting beside me in an attitude of patient dejection, gazing into the bottom of his hat; but at that moment he rose, and stretching his stiffened legs, said, mildly: 'Hadn't we better be going? There doesn't seem to be much to see here, and you know the table d'hote dinner is at half-past six o'clock.'"

Her recital ended, there was an interval of silence; then the Spirit of Life said: "There is a compensation in store for such needs as you have expressed."

"Oh, then you *do* understand?" she exclaimed. "Tell me what compensation, I entreat you!"

"It is ordained," the Spirit answered, "that every soul which seeks in vain on earth for a kindred soul to whom it can lay bare its inmost being shall find that soul here and be united to it for eternity."

A glad cry broke from her lips. "Ah, shall I find him at last?" she cried, exultant.

"He is here," said the Spirit of Life.

She looked up and saw that a man stood near whose soul (for in that unwonted light she seemed to see his soul more clearly than his face) drew her toward him with an invincible force.

"Are you really he?" she murmured.

"I am he," he answered.

She laid her hand in his and drew him toward the parapet which overhung the valley.

"Shall we go down together," she asked him, "into that marvellous country; shall we see it together, as if with the self-same eyes, and tell each other in the same words all that we think and feel?"

"So," he replied, "have I hoped and dreamed."

"What?" she asked, with rising joy. "Then you, too, have looked for me?"

"All my life."

"How wonderful! And did you never, never find anyone in the other world who understood you?"

"Not wholly—not as you and I understand each other."

"Then you feel it, too? Oh, I am happy," she sighed.

They stood, hand in hand, looking down over the parapet upon the shimmering landscape which stretched forth beneath them into sapphirine space, and the Spirit of Life, who kept watch near the threshold, heard now and then a floating fragment of their talk blown backward like the stray swallows which the wind sometimes separates from their migratory tribe.

"Did you never feel at sunset—"

"Ah, yes; but I never heard anyone else say so. Did you?"

"Do you remember that line in the third canto of *The Inferno*?"

"Ah, that line—my favorite always. Is it possible—"

"You know the stooping Victory in the frieze of the Nike Apteros?"

"You mean the one who is tying her sandal? Then you have noticed, too, that all Botticelli and Mantegna are dormant in those flying folds of her drapery?"

"After a storm in autumn have you never seen—"

"Yes, it is curious how certain flowers suggest certain painters—the perfume of the incarnation, Leonardo; that of the rose, Titian; the tuberose, Crivelli—"

"I never supposed that anyone else had noticed it."

"Have you never thought—"

"Oh, yes, often and often; but I never dreamed that anyone else had."

"But surely you must have felt—"

"Oh, yes, yes; and you, too—"

"How beautiful! How strange—"

Their voices rose and fell, like the murmur of two fountains answering each other across a garden full of flowers. At length, with a certain tender impatience, he turned to her and said: "Love, why should we linger here? All eternity lies before us. Let us go down into that beautiful country together and make a home for ourselves on some blue hill above the shining river."

As he spoke, the hand she had forgotten in his was suddenly withdrawn, and he felt that a cloud was passing over the radiance of her soul.

"A home," she repeated, slowly, "a home for you and me to live in for all eternity?"

"Why not, love? Am I not the soul that yours has sought?"

"Y-yes—yes, I know—but, don't you see, home would not be like home to me, unless—"

"Unless?" he wonderingly repeated.

She did not answer, but she thought to herself, with an impulse of whimsical inconsistency, "Unless you slammed the door and wore creaking boots."

But he had recovered his hold upon her hand, and by imperceptible degrees was leading her toward the shining steps which descended to the valley.

"Come, O my soul's soul," he passionately implored; "why delay a moment? Surely you feel, as I do, that eternity itself is too short to hold such bliss as ours. It seems to me that I can see our home already. Have I not always seem it in my dreams? It is white, love, is it not, with polished columns, and a sculptured cornice against the blue? Groves of laurel and oleander and thickets of roses surround it; but from the terrace where we walk at sunset, the eye looks out over woodlands and cool meadows where, deep-bowered under ancient boughs, a stream goes delicately toward the river. Indoors our favorite pictures hang upon the walls and the rooms are lined with books. Think, dear, at last we shall have time to read them all. With which shall we begin? Come, help me to choose. Shall it be *Faust* or the *Vita Nuova*, *The Tempest* or *Les Caprices de Marianne*, or the thirty-first canto of *The Paradise*, or *Epipsychidion* or 'Lycidas'? Tell me, dear, which one?"

As he spoke he saw the answer trembling joyously upon her lips; but it died in the ensuing silence, and she stood motionless, resisting the persuasion of his hand.

"What is it?" he entreated.

"Wait a moment," she said, with a strange hesitation in her voice. "Tell me first, are you quite sure of yourself? Is there no one on earth whom you sometimes remember?"

"Not since I have seen you," he replied; for, being a man, he had indeed forgotten.

Still she stood motionless, and he saw that the shadow deepened on her soul.

"Surely, love," he rebuked her, "it was not that which troubled you? For my part I have walked through Lethe. The past has melted like a cloud before the moon. I never lived until I saw you."

She made no answer to his pleadings, but at length,

rousing herself with a visible effort, she turned away from him and moved toward the Spirit of Life, who still stood near the threshold.

"I want to ask you a question," she said, in a troubled voice.

"Ask," said the Spirit.

"A little while ago," she began, slowly, "you told me that every soul which has not found a kindred soul on earth is destined to find one here."

"And have you not found one?" asked the Spirit.

"Yes; but will it be so with my husband's soul also?"

"No," answered the Spirit of Life, "for your husband imagined that he had found his soul's mate on earth in you; and for such delusions eternity itself contains no cure."

She gave a little cry. Was it of disappointment or triumph?

"Then—then what will happen to him when he comes here?"

"That I cannot tell you. Some field of activity and happiness he will doubtless find, in due measure to his capacity for being active and happy."

She interrupted, almost angrily: "He will never be happy without me."

"Do not be too sure of that," said the Spirit.

She took no notice of this, and the Spirit continued: "He will not understand you here any better than he did on earth."

"No matter," she said; "I shall be the only sufferer, for he always thought that he understood me."

"His boots will creak just as much as ever—"

"No matter."

"And he will slam the door—"

"Very likely."

"And continue to read railway novels—"

She interposed, impatiently: "Many men do worse than that."

"But you said just now," said the Spirit, "that you did not love him."

"True," she answered, simply; "but don't you understand that I shouldn't feel at home without him? It is all very well for a week or two—but for eternity! After all, I never minded the creaking of his boots, except when my head ached, and I don't suppose it will ache *here*; and he was always so sorry when he had slammed the door, only he never *could* remember not to. Besides, no one else would know how to look after him, he is so helpless. His inkstand would never be filled, and he would always be out of stamps and visiting-cards. He would never remember to have his umbrella re-covered, or to ask the price of anything before he bought it. Why, he wouldn't even know what novels to read. I always had to choose the kind he liked, with a murder or a forgery and a successful detective."

She turned abruptly to her kindred soul, who stood listening with a mien of wonder and dismay.

"Don't you see," she said, "that I can't possibly go with you?"

"But what do you intend to do?" asked the Spirit of Life.

"What do I intend to do?" she returned, indignantly. "Why, I mean to wait for my husband, of course. If he had come here first *he* would have waited for me for years and years; and it would break his heart not to find me here when he comes." She pointed with a contemptuous gesture to the magic vision of hill and vale sloping away to the translucent mountains. "He wouldn't give a fig for all that," she said, "if he didn't find me here."

"But consider," warned the Spirit, "that you are now choosing for eternity. It is a solemn moment."

"Choosing!" she said, with a half-sad smile. "Do you still keep up here that old fiction about choosing? I should have thought that *you* knew better than that. How can I help myself? He will expect to find me here when he comes, and he would never believe you if you told him that I had gone away with someone else— never, never."

"So be it," said the Spirit. "Here, as on earth, each one must decide for himself."

She turned to her kindred soul and looked at him gently, almost wistfully. "I am sorry," she said. "I should have liked to talk with you again; but you will under-stand, I know, and I dare say you will find someone else a great deal cleverer—"

And without pausing to hear his answer she waved him a swift farewell and turned back toward the threshold.

"Will my husband come soon?" she asked the Spirit of Life.

"That you are not destined to know," the Spirit replied.

"No matter," she said, cheerfully; "I have all eternity to wait in."

And still seated alone on the threshold, she listens for the creaking of his boots.

Katherine Mansfield

1888–1923

1858-1923

Feuille d'Album

He really was an impossible person. Too shy altogether. With absolutely nothing to say for himself. And such a weight. Once he was in your studio he never knew when to go, but would sit on and on until you nearly screamed, and burned to throw something enormous after him when he did finally blush his way out—something like the tortoise stove. The strange thing was that at first sight he looked most interesting. Everybody agreed about that. You would drift into the café one evening and there you would see, sitting in a corner, with a glass of coffee in front of him, a thin, dark boy, wearing a blue jersey with a little grey flannel jacket buttoned over it. And somehow that blue jersey and the grey jacket with the sleeves that were too short gave him the air of a boy that has made up his mind to run away to sea. Who has run away, in fact, and will get up in a moment and sling a knotted handkerchief containing his nightshirt and his mother's picture on the end of a stick, and walk out into the night and be drowned. . . . Stumble over the wharf edge on his way to the ship, even. . . . He had black close-cropped hair, grey eyes with long lashes, white cheeks and a mouth pouting as though he were determined not to cry. . . . How could one resist him? Oh, one's heart was wrung at sight. And, as if that were not enough, there was his trick of blushing. . . . Whenever the waiter came near him he turned crimson—he might have been just out of prison and the waiter in the know. . . .

"Who is he, my dear? Do you know?"

"Yes. His name is Ian French. Painter. Awfully clever, they say. Someone started by giving him a mother's tender care. She asked him how often he heard from home, whether he had enough blankets on his bed, how much milk he drank a day. But when she went round to his studio to give an eye to his socks, she rang and rang, and though she could have sworn she heard someone breathing inside, the door was not answered. . . . Hopeless!"

Someone else decided that he ought to fall in love. She summoned him to her side, called him "boy," leaned over him so that he might smell the enchanting perfume of her hair, took his arm, told him how marvellous life could be if one only had the courage, and went round to his studio one evening and rang and rang. . . . Hopeless.

"What the poor boy really wants is thoroughly rousing," said a third. So off they went to cafés and cabarets, little dances, places where you drank something that tasted like tinned apricot juice, but cost twenty-seven shillings a bottle and was called champagne, other places, too thrilling for words, where you sat in the most awful gloom, and where some one had always been shot the night before. But he did not turn a hair. Only once he got very drunk, but instead of blossoming forth, there he sat, stony, with two spots of red on his cheeks, like, my dear, yes, the dead image of that ragtime thing they were playing, like a "Broken Doll." But when she took him back to his studio he had quite recovered, and said "good night" to her in the street below, as though they had walked home from church together. . . . Hopeless.

After heaven knows how many more attempts—for the spirit of kindness dies very hard in women—they gave him up. Of course, they were still perfectly charming, and asked him to their shows, and spoke to him in the café, but that was all. When one is an artist one has no time simply for people who won't respond. Has one?

"And besides I really think there must be something rather fishy somewhere . . . don't you? It can't all be as innocent as it looks! Why come to Paris if you want to be a daisy in the field? No, I'm not suspicious. But—"

He lived at the top of a tall mournful building overlooking the river. One of those buildings that look so romantic on rainy nights and moonlight nights, when the shutters are shut, and the heavy door, and the sign advertising "a little apartment to let immediately" gleams forlorn beyond words. One of those buildings that smell so unromantic all the year round, and where the concierge lives in a glass cage on the ground floor, wrapped up in a filthy shawl, stirring something in a saucepan and ladling out tit-bits to the swollen old dog lolling on a bead cushion. . . . Perched up in the air the studio had a wonderful view. The two big windows faced the water; he could see the boats and the barges swinging up and down, and the fringe of an island planted with trees, like a round bouquet. The side window looked across to another house, shabbier still and smaller, and down below there was a flower market. You could see the tops of huge umbrellas, with frills of bright flowers escaping from them, booths covered with striped awning where they sold plants in boxes and clumps of wet gleaming palms in terra-cotta jars. Among the flowers the old women scuttled from side to side, like crabs. Really there was no need for him to go out. If he sat at the window until his white beard fell over the sill he still would have found something to draw. . . .

How surprised those tender women would have been if they had managed to force the door. For he kept his studio as neat as a pin. Everything was arranged to form a pattern, a little "still life" as it were—the saucepans with their lids on the wall behind the gas stove, the bowl of eggs, milk jug and teapot on the shelf, the books and the lamp with the crinkly paper shade on the table. An Indian curtain that had a fringe of red leopards marching round it covered his bed by day, and on the wall beside the bed on a level with your eyes when you were lying down there was a small neatly printed notice: GET UP AT ONCE.

Every day was much the same. While the light was good he slaved at his painting, then cooked his meals and tidied up the place. And in the evenings he went off to the café, or sat at home reading or making out the most complicated list of expenses headed: "What I ought to be able to do it on," and ending with a sworn statement . . . "I swear not to exceed this amount for next month. Signed, Ian French."

Nothing very fishy about this; but those far-seeing women were quite right. It wasn't all.

One evening he was sitting at the side window eating some prunes and throwing the stones on to the tops of the huge umbrellas in the deserted flower market. It had been raining—the first real spring rain of the year had fallen—a bright spangle hung on everything, and the air smelled of buds and moist earth. Many voices sounding languid and content rang out in the dusky air, and the people who had come to close their windows and fasten the shutters leaned out instead. Down below in the market the trees were peppered with new green. What kind of trees were they? he wondered. And now came the lamplighter. He stared at the house across the way, the small, shabby house, and suddenly, as if in answer to his gaze, two wings of windows opened and a girl came out on to the tiny balcony carrying a pot of daffodils. She was a strangely thin girl in a dark pinafore, with a pink handkerchief tied over her hair. Her sleeves were rolled up almost to her shoulders and her slender arms shone against the dark stuff.

"Yes, it is quite warm enough. It will do them good," she said, putting down the pot and turning to some one in the room inside. As she turned she put her hands up to the handkerchief and tucked away some wisps of hair. She looked down at the deserted market and up at the sky, but where he sat there might have been a hollow in the air. She simply did not see the house opposite. And then she disappeared.

His heart fell out of the side window of his studio, and down to the balcony of the house opposite—buried itself in the pot of daffodils under the half-opened buds and spears of green. . . . That room with the balcony was the sitting-room, and the one next door to it was the kitchen. He heard the clatter of the dishes as she washed up after supper, and then she came to the window, knocked a little mop against the ledge, and hung it on a nail to dry. She never sang or unbraided her hair, or held out her arms to the moon as young girls are supposed to do. And she always wore the same dark pinafore and the pink handkerchief over her hair. . . . Whom did she live with? Nobody else came to those two windows, and yet she was always talking to some one in the room. Her mother, he decided, was an invalid. They took in sewing. The father was dead. . . . He had been a journalist—very pale, with long moustaches, and a piece of black hair falling over his forehead.

By working all day they just made enough money to live on, but they never went out and they had no friends. Now when he sat down at his table he had to make an entirely new set of sworn statements. . . . Not to go to the side window before a certain hour: signed, Ian French. Not to think about her until he had put away his painting things for the day: signed, Ian French.

It was quite simple. She was the only person he really wanted to know, because she was, he decided, the only other person alive who was just his age. He couldn't stand giggling girls, and he had no use for grown-up women. . . . She was his age, she was—well, just like him. He sat in his dusky studio, tired, with one arm hanging over the back of his chair, staring in at her window and seeing himself in there with her. She had a violent temper; they quarrelled terribly at times, he and she. She had a way of stamping her foot and twisting her hands in her pinafore . . . furious. And she very rarely laughed. Only when she told him about an absurd little kitten she once had who used to roar and pretend to be a lion when it was given meat to eat. Things like that made her laugh. . . . But as a rule they sat together very quietly; he, just as he was sitting now, and she with her hands folded in her lap and her feet tucked under, talking in low tones, or silent and tired after the day's work. Of course, she never asked him about his pictures, and of course he made the most wonderful drawings of her which she hated, because he made her so thin and so dark. . . . But how could he get to know her? This might go on for years. . . .

Then he discovered that once a week, in the evenings, she went out shopping. On two successive Thursdays she came to the window wearing an old-fashioned cape over the pinafore, and carrying a basket. From where he sat he could not see the door of her house, but on the next Thursday evening at the same time he snatched up his cap and ran down the stairs. There was a lovely pink light over everything. He saw it glowing in the river, and the people walking towards him had pink faces and pink hands.

He leaned against the side of his house waiting for her and he had no idea of what he was going to do or say. "Here she comes," said a voice in his head. She walked very quickly, with small, light steps; with one hand she carried the basket, with the other she kept the cape together. . . . What could he do? He could only follow. . . . First she went into the grocer's and spent a long time in there, and then she went into the butcher's where she had to wait her turn. Then she was an age at the draper's matching something, and then she went to the fruit shop and bought a lemon. As he watched her he knew more surely than ever he must get to know her, now. Her composure, her seriousness and her loneliness, the very way she walked as though she was eager to be done with this world of grown-ups all was so natural to him and so inevitable.

"Yes, she is always like that," he thought proudly. "We have nothing to do with these people."

But now she was on her way home and he was as far off as ever. . . . She suddenly turned into the dairy and he saw her through the window buying an egg. She picked it out of the basket with such care—a brown one, a beautifully shaped one, the one he would have chosen. And when she came out of the dairy he went in after her. In a moment he was out again, and following her past his house across the flower market, dodging among the huge umbrellas and treading on the fallen flowers and the round marks where the pots had stood. . . . Through her door he crept, and up the stairs after, taking care to tread in time with her so that she should not notice.

Finally, she stopped on the landing, and took the key out of her purse. As she put it into the door he ran up and faced her.

Blushing more crimson than ever, but looking at her severely he said, almost angrily: "Excuse me, Mademoiselle, you dropped this."

And he handed her an egg.

Mr. and Mrs. Dove

Of course he knew—no man better—that he hadn't a ghost of a chance, he hadn't an earthly. The very idea of such a thing was preposterous. So preposterous that he'd perfectly understand it if her father—well, whatever her father chose to do he'd perfectly understand. In fact, nothing short of desperation, nothing short of the fact that this was positively his last day in England for God knows how long, would have screwed him up to it. And even now . . . He chose a tie out of the chest of drawers, a blue and cream check tie, and sat on the side of his bed. Supposing she replied, "What impertinence!" would he be surprised? Not in the least, he decided, turning up his soft collar and turning it down over the tie. He expected her to say something like that. He didn't see, if he looked at the affair dead soberly, what else she could say.

Here he was! And nervously he tied a bow in front of the mirror, jammed his hair down with both hands, pulled out the flaps of his jacket pockets. Making between £500 and £600 a year on a fruit farm in—of all places—Rhodesia. No capital. Not a penny coming to him. No chance of his income increasing for at least four years. As for looks and all that sort of thing, he was completely out of the running. He couldn't even boast of top-hole health, for the East Africa business had knocked him out so thoroughly that he'd had to take six months' leave. He was still fearfully pale— worse even than usual this afternoon, he thought, bending forward and peering into the mirror. Good heavens! What had happened? His hair looked almost bright green. Dash it all, he hadn't green hair at all events. That was a bit too steep. And then the green light trembled in the glass; it was the shadow from the tree outside. Reggie turned away, took out his cigarette case, but remembering how the mater hated him to smoke in his bedroom, put it back again and drifted over to the chest of drawers. No, he was dashed if he could think of one blessed thing in his favour, while she . . . Ah! . . . He stopped dead, folded his arms, and leaned hard against the chest of drawers.

And in spite of her position, her father's wealth, the fact that she was an only child and far and away the most popular girl in the neighbourhood; in spite of her beauty and her cleverness—cleverness!—it was a great deal more than that, there was really nothing she couldn't do; he fully believed, had it been necessary, she would have been a genius at anything—in spite of the fact that her parents adored her, and she them, and they'd as soon let her go all that way as . . . In spite of every single thing you could think of, so terrific was his love that he couldn't help hoping. Well, was it hope? Or was this queer, timid longing to have the chance of looking after her, of making it his job to see that she had everything she wanted, and that nothing came near her that wasn't perfect—just love? How he loved her! He squeezed hard against the chest of drawers and murmured to it, "I love her, I love her!" And just for the moment he was with her on the way to Umtali. It was night. She sat in a corner asleep. Her soft chin was tucked into her soft collar, her gold-brown lashes lay on her cheeks. He doted on her delicate little nose, her perfect lips, her ear like a baby's, and the gold-brown curl that half covered it. They were passing through the jungle. It was warm and dark and far away. Then she woke up and said, "Have I been asleep?" and he answered, "Yes. Are you all right? Here, let me—" And he leaned forward to . . . He bent over her. This was such bliss that he could dream no further. But it gave him the courage to bound downstairs, to snatch his straw hat from the hall, and to say as he closed the front door, "Well, I can only try my luck, that's all."

But his luck gave him a nasty jar, to say the least, almost immediately. Promenading up and down the garden path with Chinny and Biddy, the ancient Pekes, was the mater. Of course Reginald was fond of the mater and all that. She—she meant well, she had no end of grit, and so on. But there was no denying it, she was rather a grim parent. And there had been moments, many of them, in Reggie's life, before Uncle Alick died and left him the fruit farm, when he was convinced that to be a widow's only son was about the worst punishment a chap could have. And what made it rougher than ever was that she was positively all that he had. She wasn't only a combined parent, as it were, but she had quarrelled with all her own and the governor's relations before Reggie had won his first trouser pockets. So that whenever Reggie was homesick out there, sitting on his dark veranda by starlight, while the gramophone cried, "Dear, what is Life but Love?" his only vision was of the mater, tall and stout, rustling down the garden path, with Chinny and Biddy at her heels . . .

The mater, with her scissors outspread to snap the head of a dead something or other, stopped at the sight of Reggie.

"You are not going out, Reginald?" she asked, seeing that he was.

"I'll be back for tea, mater," said Reggie weakly, plunging his hands into his jacket pockets.

Snip. Off came a head. Reggie almost jumped.

"I should have thought you could have spared your mother your last afternoon," said she.

Silence. The Pekes stared. They understood every word of the mater's. Biddy lay down with her tongue poked out; she was so fat and glossy she looked like a lump of half-melted toffee. But Chinny's porcelain eyes gloomed at Reginald, and he sniffed faintly, as though the whole world were one unpleasant smell. Snip, went the scissors again. Poor little beggars; they were getting it!

"And where are you going, if your mother may ask?" asked the mater.

It was over at last, but Reggie did not slow down until he was out of sight of the house and half-way to Colonel Proctor's. Then only he noticed what a top-hole afternoon it was. It had been raining all the morning, late summer rain, warm, heavy, quick, and now the sky was clear, except for a long tail of little clouds, like duckings, sailing over the forest. There was just enough wind to shake the last drops off the trees; one warm star splashed on his hand. Ping!—another drummed on his hat. The empty road gleamed, the hedges smelled of briar, and how big and bright the hollyhocks glowed in the cottage gardens. And here was Colonel Proctor's—here it was already. His hand was on the gate, his elbow jogged the syringa bushes, and petals and pollen scattered over his coat sleeve. But wait a bit. This was too quick altogether. He'd meant to think the whole thing out again. Here, steady. But he was walking up the path, with the huge rose bushes on either side. It can't be done like this. But his hand had grasped the bell, given it a pull, and started it pealing wildly, as if he'd come to say the house was on fire. The housemaid must have been in the hall, too, for the front door flashed open, and Reggie was shut in the empty drawing-room before that confounded bell had stopped ringing. Strangely enough, when it did, the big room, shadowy, with some one's parasol lying on top of the grand piano, bucked him up—or rather, excited him. It was so quiet, and yet in one moment the door would open, and his fate be decided. The feeling was not unlike that of being at the dentist's; he was almost reckless. But at the same time, to his immense surprise, Reggie heard himself saying, "Lord, Thou knowest, Thou hast not done *much* for me. . . ." That pulled him up; that made him realize again how dead serious it was. Too late. The door handle turned. Anne came in, crossed the shadowy space between them, gave him her hand, and said, in her small, soft voice, "I'm so sorry, father is out. And mother is having a day in town, hat-hunting. There's only me to entertain you, Reggie."

Reggie gasped, pressed his own hat to his jacket buttons, and stammered out, "As a matter of fact, I've only come . . . to say good-bye."

"Oh!" cried Anne softly—she stepped back from him and her grey eyes danced—"What a *very* short visit!"

Then, watching him, her chin tilted, she laughed outright, a long, soft peal, and walked away from him over to the piano, and leaned against it, playing with the tassel of the parasol.

"I'm so sorry," she said, "to be laughing like this. I don't know why I do. It's just a bad ha-habit." And suddenly she stamped her grey shoe, and took a pocket-handkerchief out of her white woolly jacket. "I really must conquer it, it's too absurd," said she.

"Good heavens, Anne," cried Reggie, "I love to hear you laughing! I can't imagine anything more—"

But the truth was, and they both knew it, she wasn't always laughing; it wasn't really a habit. Only ever since the day they'd met, ever since that very first moment, for some strange reason that Reggie wished to God he understood, Anne had laughed at him. Why? It didn't matter where they were or what they were talking about. They might begin by being as serious as possible, dead serious—at any rate, as far as he was concerned—but then suddenly, in the middle of a sentence, Anne would glance at him, and a little quick quiver passed over her face. Her lips parted, her eyes danced, and she began laughing.

Another queer thing about it was, Reggie had an idea she didn't herself know why she laughed. He had seen her turn away, frown, suck in her cheeks, press her hands together. But it was no use. The long, soft peal sounded, even while she cried, "I don't know why I'm laughing." It was a mystery. . . .

Now she tucked the handkerchief away.

"Do sit down," said she. "And smoke, won't you? There are cigarettes in that little box beside you. I'll have one too." He lighted a match for her, and as she bent forward he saw the tiny flame glow in the pearl ring she wore. "It is to-morrow that you're going, isn't it?" said Anne.

"Yes, to-morrow as ever was," said Reggie, and he blew a little fan of smoke. Why on earth was he so nervous? Nervous wasn't the word for it.

"It's—it's frightfully hard to believe," he added.

"Yes—isn't it?" said Anne softly, and she leaned forward and rolled the point of her cigarette round the green ash-tray. How beautiful she looked like that!—simply beautiful—and she was so small in that immense chair. Reginald's heart swelled with tenderness, but it was her voice, her soft voice, that made him tremble. "I feel you've been here for years," she said.

Reginald took a deep breath of his cigarette. "It's ghastly, this idea of going back," he said.

"Coo-roo-coo-coo-coo," sounded from the quiet.

"But you're fond of being out there, aren't you?" said Anne. She hooked her finger through her pearl necklace. "Father was saying only the other night how lucky he thought you were to have a life of your own." And she looked up at him. Reginald's smile was rather wan. "I don't feel fearfully lucky," he said lightly.

"*Roo-coo-coo-coo,*" came again. And Anne murmured, "You mean it's lonely."

"Oh, it isn't the loneliness I care about," said Reginald, and he stumped his cigarette savagely on the green ash-tray. "I could stand any amount of it, used to like it even. It's the idea of—" Suddenly, to his horror, he felt himself blushing.

"*Roo-coo-coo-coo! Roo-coo-coo-coo!*"

Anne jumped up. "Come and say good-bye to my doves," she said. "They've been moved to the side veranda. You do like doves, don't you, Reggie?"

"Awfully," said Reggie, so fervently that as he opened the French window for her and stood to one side, Anne ran forward and laughed at the doves instead.

To and fro, to and fro over the fine red sand on the floor of the dove house, walked the two doves. One was always in front of the other. One ran forward, uttering a little cry, and the other followed, solemnly bowing and bowing. "You see," explained Anne, "the one in front, she's Mrs. Dove. She looks at Mr. Dove and gives that little laugh and runs forward, and he follows her, bowing and bowing. And that makes her laugh again.

Away she runs, and after her," cried Anne, and she sat back on her heels, "comes poor Mr. Dove, bowing and bowing . . . and that's their whole life. They never do anything else, you know." She got up and took some yellow grains out of a bag on the roof of the dove house. "When you think of them, out in Rhodesia, Reggie, you can be sure that is what they will be doing. . . ."

Reggie gave no sign of having seen the doves or of having heard a word. For the moment he was conscious only of the immense effort it took to tear his secret out of himself and offer it to Anne. "Anne, do you think you could ever care for me?" It was done. It was over. And in the little pause that followed Reginald saw the garden open to the light, the blue quivering sky, the flutter of leaves on the veranda poles, and Anne turning over the grains of maize on her palm with one finger. Then slowly she shut her hand, and the new world faded as she murmured slowly, "No, never in that way." But he had scarcely time to feel anything before she walked quickly away, and he followed her down the steps, along the garden path, under the pink rose arches, across the lawn. There, with the gay herbaceous border behind her, Anne faced Reginald. "It isn't that I'm not awfully fond of you," she said. "I am. But"—her eyes widened—"Not in the way"—a quiver passed over her face—"One ought to be fond of—" Her lips parted, and she couldn't stop herself. She began laughing. "There, you see, you see," she cried, "it's your check t-tie. Even at this moment, when one would think one really would be solemn, your tie reminds me fearfully of the bow-tie that cats wear in pictures! Oh, please forgive me for being so horrid, please!"

Reggie caught hold of her little warm hand. "There's no question of forgiving you," he said quickly. "How could there be? And I do believe I know why I make you laugh. It's because you're so far above me in every way that I am somehow ridiculous. I see that, Anne. But if I were to—"

"No, no." Anne squeezed his hand hard. "It's not that. That's all wrong. I'm not far above you at all. You're much better than I am. You're marvellously unselfish and . . . and kind and simple. I'm none of those things. You don't know me. I'm the most awful character," said Anne. "Please don't interrupt. And besides, that's not the

127

point. The point is"—she shook her head—"I couldn't possibly marry a man I laughed at. Surely you see that. The man I marry—" breathed Anne softly. She broke off. She drew her hand away, and looking at Reggie she smiled strangely, dreamily. "The man I marry—"

And it seemed to Reggie that a tall, handsome, brilliant stranger stepped in front of him and took his place—the kind of man that Anne and he had seen often at the theatre, walking on to the stage from nowhere, without a word catching the heroine in his arms, and after one long, tremendous look, carrying her off to anywhere. . . .

Reggie bowed to his vision. "Yes, I see," he said huskily.

"Do you?" said Anne. "Oh, I do hope you do. Because I feel so horrid about it. It's so hard to explain. You know I've never—" She stopped. Reggie looked at her. She was smiling. "Isn't it funny?" she said. "I can say anything to you. I always have been able to from the very beginning."

He tried to smile, to say "I'm glad." She went on. "I've never known anyone I like as much as I like you.

I've never felt so happy with anyone. But I'm sure it's not what people and what books mean when they talk about love. Do you understand? Oh, if you only knew how horrid I feel. But we'd be like . . . like Mr. and Mrs. Dove."

That did it. That seemed to Reginald final, and so terribly true that he could hardly bear it. "Don't drive it home," he said, and he turned away from Anne and looked across the lawn. There was the gardener's cottage, with the dark ilex-tree beside it. A wet, blue thumb of transparent smoke hung above the chimney. It didn't look real. How his throat ached! Could he speak? He had a shot. "I must be getting along home," he croaked, and he began walking across the lawn. But Anne ran after him. "No, don't. You can't go yet," she said imploringly. "You can't possibly go away feeling like that." And she stared up at him frowning, biting her lip.

"Oh, that's all right," said Reggie, giving himself a shake. "I'll . . . I'll—" And he waved his hand as much to say "get over it."

"But this is awful," said Anne. She clasped her hands and stood in front of him. "Surely you do see how fatal it would be for us to marry, don't you?"

"Oh, quite, quite," said Reggie, looking at her with haggard eyes.

"How wrong, how wicked, feeling as I do. I mean, it's all very well for Mr. and Mrs. Dove. But imagine that in real life—imagine it!"

"Oh, absolutely," said Reggie, and he started to walk on. But again Anne stopped him. She tugged at his sleeve, and to his astonishment, this time, instead of laughing, she looked like a little girl who was going to cry.

"Then why, if you understand, are you so un-unhappy?" she wailed. "Why do you mind so fearfully? Why do you look so aw-awful?"

Reggie gulped, and again he waved something away. "I can't help it," he said, "I've had a blow. If I cut off now, I'll be able to—"

"How can you talk of cutting off now?" said Anne scornfully. She stamped her foot at Reggie; she was crimson. "How can you be so cruel? I can't let you go until I know for certain that you are just as happy as you were before you asked me to marry you. Surely you must see that, it's so simple."

But it did not seem at all simple to Reginald. It seemed impossibly difficult.

"Even if I can't marry you, how can I know that you're all that way away, with only that awful mother to write to, and that you're miserable, and that it's all my fault?"

"It's not your fault. Don't think that. It's just fate." Reggie took her hand off his sleeve and kissed it. "Don't pity me, dear little Anne," he said gently. And this time he nearly ran, under the pink arches, along the garden path.

"Roo-coo-coo-coo! Roo-coo-coo-coo!" sounded from the veranda. "Reggie, Reggie," from the garden.

He stopped, he turned. But when she saw his timid, puzzled look, she gave a little laugh.

"Come back, Mr. Dove," said Anne. And Reginald came slowly across the lawn.

L. M. Montgomery

1874–1942

The Tryst of the White Lady

"I wisht ye'd git married, Roger," said Catherine Ames. "I'm gitting too old to work—seventy last April—and who's going to look after ye when I'm gone. Git married, b'y—git married."

Roger Temple winced. His aunt's harsh, disagreeable voice always jarred horribly on his sensitive nerves. He was fond of her after a fashion, but always that voice made him wonder if there could be anything harder to endure.

Then he gave a bitter little laugh.

"Who'd have me, Aunt Catherine?" he asked.

Catherine Ames looked at him critically across the supper table. She loved him in her way, with all her heart, but she was not in the least blind to his defects. She did not mince matters with herself or with other people. Roger was a sallow, plain-featured fellow, small and insignificant looking. And, as if this were not bad enough, he walked with a slight limp and had one thin shoulder a little higher than the other—"Jarback" Temple he had been called in school, and the name still clung to him. To be sure, he had very fine grey eyes, but their dreamy brilliance gave his dull face an uncanny look which girls did not like, and so made matters rather worse than better. Of course looks didn't matter so much in the case of a man; Steve Millar was homely enough, and all marked up with smallpox to boot, yet he had got for wife the prettiest and smartest girl in South Bay. But Steve was rich. Roger was poor and always would be. He worked his stony little farm, from which his father and grandfather had wrested a fair living, after a fashion, but Nature had not cut him out for a successful farmer. He hadn't the strength for it and his heart wasn't in it. He'd rather be hanging over a book. Catherine secretly thought Roger's matrimonial chances very poor, but it would not do to discourage the b'y. What he needed was spurring on.

"Ye'll git someone if ye don't fly too high," she announced loudly and cheerfully. "Thar's always a gal or two here and thar that's glad to marry for a home. 'Tain't no use for *you* to be settin' your thoughts on anyone young and pretty. Ye wouldn't git her and ye'd be worse off if ye did. Your grandfather married for looks, and a nice useless wife he got—sick half her time. Git a good strong girl that ain't afraid of work, that'll hold things together when ye're reading po'try—that's as much as you kin expect. And the sooner the better. I'm done—last winter's rheumatiz has about finished *me*. An' we can't afford hired help."

Roger felt as if his raw, quivering soul were being seared. He looked at his aunt curiously—at her broad, flat face with the mole on the end of her dumpy nose, the bristling hairs on her chin, the wrinkled yellow neck, the pale, protruding eyes, the coarse, good-humoured mouth. She was so extremely ugly—and he had seen her across the table all his life. For twenty-five years he had looked at her so. Must he continue to go on looking at ugliness in the shape of a wife all the rest of his life—he, who worshipped beauty in everything?

"Did my mother look like you, Aunt Catherine?" he asked abruptly.

His aunt stared—and snorted. Her snort was meant to express kindly amusement, but it sounded like derision and contempt.

"Yer ma wasn't so humly as me," she said cheerfully, "but she wan't no beauty either. None of the Temples was ever better lookin' than was necessary. We was *workers*. Yer pa wa'n't bad looking. You're humlier than either of 'em. Some ways ye take after yer grandma—though *she* was counted pretty at one time. She was yaller and spindlin' like you, and you've got her eyes. What yer so int'rested in yer ma's looks all at once fer?"

"I was wondering," said Roger coolly, "if Father ever looked at her across the table and wished she were prettier."

Catherine giggled. Her giggle was ugly and disagreeable like everything else about her—everything except a certain odd, loving, loyal old heart buried deep in her bosom, for the sake of which Roger endured the giggle and all the rest.

"Dessay he did—dessay he did. Men al'ays has a hankerin' for good looks. But ye've got to cut yer coat 'cording to yer cloth. As for yer poor ma, she didn't live long enough to git as ugly as me. When I come here to keep house for yer pa, folks said as it wouldn't be long 'fore he married me. *I* wouldn't a-minded. But yer pa never hinted it. S'pose he'd had enough of ugly women likely."

Catherine snorted amiably again. Roger got up—he couldn't endure any more just then. He must escape.

"Now you think over what I've said," his aunt called after him. "Ye've gotter git a wife soon, however ye manage it. 'Twon't be so hard if ye're reasonable. Don't stay out as late as ye did last night. Ye coughed all night. Where was ye—down at the shore?"

"No," said Roger, who always answered her questions even when he hated to. "I was down at Aunt Isabel's grave."

"Till eleven o'clock! Ye ain't wise! I dunno what hankering ye have after that unchancy place. *I* ain't been near it for twenty year. I wonder ye ain't scairt. What'd ye think ye'd do if ye saw her ghost?"

Catherine looked curiously at Roger. She was very superstitious and she believed firmly in ghosts, and saw no absurdity in her question.

"I wish I *could* see it," said Roger, his great eyes flashing. He believed in ghosts too, at least in Isabel Temple's ghost. His uncle had seen it; his grandfather had seen it; he believed he would see it—the beautiful, bewitching, mocking, luring ghost of lovely Isabel Temple.

"Don't wish such stuff," said Catherine. "Nobody ain't never the same after they've seen her."

"Was Uncle different?" Roger had come back into the kitchen and was looking curiously at his aunt.

"Diff'rent? He was another man. He didn't even *look* the same. Sich eyes! Al'ays looking past ye at something behind ye. They'd give anyone creeps. He never had any notion of flesh-and-blood women after that— said a man wouldn't, after seeing Isabel. His life was plumb ruined. Lucky he died young. I hated to be in the same room with him—he wa'n't canny, that was all there was to it. *You* keep away from that grave—*you* don't want to look odder than ye are by nature. And when ye git married, ye'll have to give up roamin' about half the night in graveyards. A wife wouldn't put up with it, as I've done."

"I'll never get as good a wife as you, Aunt Catherine," said Roger with a little whimsical smile that gave him the look of an amused gnome.

"Dessay you won't. But someone ye have to have. Why'n't ye try 'Liza Adams. She *might* have ye—she's gittin' on."

"'Liza . . . Adams!"

"That's what I said. Ye needn't repeat it— 'Liza . . . Adams—'s if I'd mentioned a hippopotamus. I git out of patience with ye. I b'lieve in my heart ye think ye ought to git a wife that'd look like a picter."

"I do, Aunt Catherine. That's just the kind of wife I want—grace and beauty and charm. Nothing less than that will ever content me."

Roger laughed bitterly again and went out. It was sunset. There was no work to do that night except to milk the cows, and his little home boy could do that. He felt a glad freedom. He put his hand in his pocket to see if his beloved Wordsworth was there and then he took his way across the fields, under a sky of purple and amber, walking quickly despite his limp. He wanted to get to some solitary place where he could forget Aunt Catherine and her abominable suggestions and escape into the world of dreams where he habitually lived and where he found the loveliness he had not found nor could hope to find in his real world.

Roger's mother had died when he was three and his father when he was eight. His little, old, bedridden grandmother had lived until he was twelve. He had loved her passionately. She had not been pretty in his remembrance—a tiny, shrunken, wrinkled thing—but she had beautiful grey eyes that never grew old and a soft, gentle voice—the only woman's voice he had ever heard with pleasure. He was very critical as regards women's voices and very sensitive to them. Nothing hurt him quite so much as an unlovely voice—not even unloveliness of face. Her death had left him desolate. She was the only human being who had ever understood him. He could never, he thought, have got through his tortured school days without her. After she died he would not go to school. He was not in any sense educated. His father and grandfather had been illiterate men and he had inherited their underdeveloped brain cells. But he loved poetry and read all he could get of it. It overlaid his primitive nature with a curious iridescence of fancy and furnished him with ideals and hungers his environment could never satisfy. He loved beauty in everything. Moonrises hurt him with their loveliness and he could sit for hours gazing at a white narcissus—much to his aunt's exasperation. He was solitary by nature. He felt horribly alone in a crowded building but never in the woods or in the wild places along the shore. It was because of this that his aunt could not get him to go to church—which was a horror to her orthodox soul. He told her he would like to go to church if it were empty but he could not bear it when it was full—full of smug, ugly people. Most people, he thought, were ugly—though not so ugly as he was—and ugliness made him sick with repulsion. Now and then he saw a pretty girl at whom he liked to look but he never saw one that wholly pleased him. To him, the homely, crippled, poverty-stricken Roger Temple whom they all would have scorned, there was always a certain subtle something wanting, and the lack of it kept him heartwhole. He knew that this probably saved him from much suffering, but for all that he regretted it. He wanted to love, even vainly; he wanted to experience this passion of which the poets sang so much. Without it he felt he lacked the key to a world of wonder. He even tried to fall in love; he went to church for several Sundays and sat where he could see beautiful Elsa Carey. She was lovely—it gave him pleasure to look at her; the gold of her hair was so bright and living; the pink of her cheek so pure, the curve of her neck so flawless, the lashes of her eyes so dark and silken. But he looked at her as at a picture. When he tried to think and dream of her, it bored him. Besides, he knew she had a rather nasal voice. He used to laugh sarcastically to himself over Elsa's feelings if she had known how desperately he was trying to fall in love with her and failing—Elsa the queen of hearts, who believed she had only to look to reign. He gave up trying at last, but he still longed to love. He knew he would never marry; he could not marry plainness, and beauty would have none of him; but he did not want to miss everything and he had moments when he was very bitter and rebellious because he felt he must miss it forever.

He went straight to Isabel Temple's grave in the remote shore field of his farm. Isabel Temple had lived and died eighty years ago. She had been very lovely, very wilful, very fond of playing with the hearts of men. She had married William Temple, the brother of his great-grandfather, and as she stood in her white dress beside her bridegroom, at the conclusion of the wedding ceremony, a jilted lover, crazed by despair, had entered the house and shot her dead. She had been buried in the shore field, where a square space had been dyked off in the centre for a burial lot because the church was then so far away. With the passage of years the lot had grown up so thickly with fir and birch and wild cherry that it looked like a compact grove. A winding path led through it to its heart where Isabel Temple's grave was, thickly overgrown with long, silken, pale green grass. Roger hurried along the path and sat down on the big grey boulder by the grave, looking about him with a long breath of delight. How lovely—and witching—and unearthly it was here. Little ferns were growing in the hollows and cracks of the big boulder where clay had lodged. Over Isabel Temple's crooked, lichened gravestone hung a young wild cherry in its delicate bloom. Above it, in a little space of sky left by the slender tree tops, was a young moon. It was too dark here after all to read Wordsworth, but that did not matter. The place, with its moist air, its tang of fir balsam, was like a perfumed room where a man might dream dreams and see visions. There was a soft murmur of wind in the boughs over him, and the faraway moan of the sea on the bar crept in. Roger surrendered himself utterly to the charm of the place. When he entered that grove, he had left behind the realm of daylight and things known and come into the realm of shadow and mystery and enchantment. Anything might happen—anything might be true.

Eighty long years had come and gone, but Isabel Temple, thus cruelly torn from life at the moment when it had promised her most, did not even yet rest calmly in her grave; such at least was the story, and Roger believed it. It was in his blood to believe it. The Temples were a superstitious family, and there was nothing in Roger's upbringing to correct the tendency. His was not a sceptical or scientific mind. He was ignorant and poetical and credulous. He had always accepted unquestioningly the tale that Isabel Temple had been seen on earth long after the red clay was heaped over her murdered body. Her bridegroom had seen her, when he went to visit her on the eve of his second and unhappy marriage; his grandfather had seen her. His grandmother, who had told him Isabel's story, had told him this too, and believed it. She had added, with a bitterness foreign to his idea of her, that her husband had never been the same to her afterwards; his uncle had seen her—and had lived and died a haunted man. It was only to men the lovely, restless ghost appeared, and her appearance boded no good to him who saw. Roger knew this, but he had a curious longing to see her. He had never avoided her grave as others of his tribe did. He loved the spot, and he believed that some time he would see Isabel

Temple there. She came, so the story went, to one in each generation of the family.

He gazed down at her sunken grave; a little wind, that came stealing along the floor of the grove, raised and swayed the long, hair-like grass on it, giving the curious suggestion of something prisoned under it trying to draw a long breath and float upward.

Then, when he lifted his eyes again, he saw her!

She was standing behind the gravestone, under the cherry tree, whose long white branches touched her head; standing there, with her head drooping a little, but looking steadily at him. It was just between dusk and dark now, but he saw her very plainly. She was dressed in white, with some filmy scarf over her head, and her hair hung in a dark heavy braid over her shoulder. Her face was small and ivory-white, and her eyes were very large and dark. Roger looked straight into them and they did something to him—drew something out of him that was never to be his again—his heart? His soul? He did not know. He only knew that lovely Isabel Temple had now come to him and that he was hers forever.

For a few moments that seemed years he looked at her—looked till the lure of her eyes drew him to his feet as a man rises in sleep-walking. As he slowly stood up, the low-hanging bough of a fir tree pushed his cap down over his face and blinded him. When he snatched it off, she was gone.

Roger Temple did not go home that night till the spring dawn was in the sky. Catherine was sleepless with anxiety about him. When she heard him come up the stairs, she opened her door and peeped out. Roger went along the hall without seeing her. His brilliant eyes stared straight before him, and there was something in his face that made Catherine steal back to her bed with a little shiver of fear. He looked like his uncle. She did not ask him, when they met at breakfast, where or how he had spent the night. He had been dreading the question and was relieved beyond measure when it was not asked. But, apart from that, he was hardly conscious of her presence. He ate and drank mechanically and voicelessly. When he had gone out, Catherine wagged her uncomely grey head ominously.

"He's bewitched," she muttered. "I know the signs. He's seen her—drat her! It's time she gave up that kind of work. Well, I dunno what to do—thar ain't anything I can do, I reckon. He'll never marry now—I'm as sure of that as of any mortal thing. He's in love with a ghost."

It had not yet occurred to Roger that he was in love. He thought of nothing but Isabel Temple—her lovely, lovely face, sweeter than any picture he had ever seen or any ideal he had dreamed, her long dark hair, her slim form and, more than all, her compelling eyes. He saw them wherever he looked—they drew him—he would have followed them to the end of the world, heedless of all else.

He longed for night, that he might again steal to the grave in the haunted grove. She might come again—who knew? He felt no fear, nothing but a terrible hunger to see her again. But she did not come that night—nor the next—nor the next. Two weeks went by and he had not seen her. Perhaps he would never see her again—the thought filled him with anguish not to be borne. He knew now that he loved her—Isabel Temple, dead for eighty years. This was love—this searing, torturing, intolerably sweet thing—this possession of body and soul and spirit. The poets had sung but weakly of it. He could tell them better if he could find words. Could other men have loved at all—could any man love those blowzy, common girls of earth? It seemed impossible—absurd. There was only one thing that could be loved—that white spirit. No wonder his uncle had died. He, Roger Temple, would soon die too. That would be well. Only the dead could woo Isabel. Meanwhile he revelled in his torment and his happiness—so madly commingled that he never knew whether he was in heaven or hell. It was beautiful—and dreadful—and wonderful—and exquisite—oh, so exquisite. Mortal love could never be so exquisite. He had never lived before—now he lived in every fibre of his being.

He was glad Aunt Catherine did not worry him with questions. He had feared she would. But she never asked any questions now and she was afraid of Roger, as she had been afraid of his uncle. She dared not ask questions. It was a thing that must not be tampered with. Who knew what she might hear if she asked him questions? She was very unhappy. Something dreadful had happened to her poor boy—he had been bewitched by that hussy—he would die as his uncle had died.

"Mebbe it's best," she muttered. "He's the last of the Temples, so mebbe she'll rest in her grave when she's killed 'em all. I dunno what she's sich a spite at *them* for—there'd be more sense if she'd haunt the Mortons, seein' as a Morton killed her. Well, I'm mighty old and tired and worn out. It don't seem that it's been much use, the way I've slaved and fussed to bring that b'y up and keep things together for him—and now the ghost's got him. I might as well have let him die when he was a sickly baby."

If this had been said to Roger he would have retorted that it was worthwhile to have lived long enough to feel what he was feeling now. He would not have missed it for a score of other men's lives. He had drunk of some immortal wine and was as a god. Even if she never came again, he had seen her once, and she had taught him life's great secret in that one unforgettable exchange of eyes.

She was his—his in spite of his ugliness and his crooked shoulder. No man could ever take her from him.

But she did come again. One evening, when the darkening grove was full of magic in the light of the rising yellow moon shining across the level field, Roger sat on the big boulder by the grave. The evening was very still; there was no sound save the echoes of noisy laughter that seemed to come up from the bay shore—drunken fishermen, likely as not. Roger resented the intrusion of such a sound in such a place—it was a sacrilege. When he came here to dream of her, only the loveliest of muted sounds should be heard—the faintest whisper of trees, the half-heard, half-felt moan of surf, the airiest sigh of wind. He never read Wordsworth now or any other book. He only sat there and thought of her, his great eyes alight, his pale face flushed with the wonder of his love.

She slipped through the dark boughs like a moonbeam and stood by the stone. Again he saw her quite plainly—saw and drank her in with his eyes. He did not feel surprise—something in him had known she would come again. He would not move a muscle lest he lose her as he had lost her before. They looked at each other—for how long? He did not know; and then—a horrible thing happened. Into that place of wonder and revelation and mystery reeled a hiccoughing, laughing creature, a drunken sailor from a harbour ship, with a leering face and desecrating breath.

"Oh, you're here, my dear—I thought I'd catch you yet," he said.

He caught hold of her. She screamed. Roger sprang forward and struck him in the face. In his fury of sudden rage the strength of ten seemed to animate his slender body and pass into his blow. The sailor reeled back and put up his hands. He was a coward—and even a brave man might have been daunted by that terrible white face and those blazing eyes. He backed down the path.

"Shorry—shorry," he muttered. "Didn't know she was your girl—shorry I butted in. Shentlemans never butt in—shorry—shir—shorry."

He kept repeating his ridiculous "shorry" until he was out of the grove. Then he turned and ran stumblingly across the field. Roger did not follow; he went back to Isabel Temple's grave. The girl was lying across it; he thought she was unconscious. He stooped and picked her up—she was light and small, but she was warm flesh and blood; she clung uncertainly to him for a moment and he felt her breath on his face. He did not speak—he was too sick at heart. She did not speak either. He did not think this strange until afterwards. He was incapable of thinking just then; he was dazed, wretched, lost. Presently he became aware that she was timidly pulling his arm. It seemed that she wanted him to go with her—she was evidently frightened of that brute—he must take her to safety. And then—

She moved on down the little path and he followed. Out in the moonlit field he saw her clearly. With her drooping head, her flowing dark hair, her great brown eyes, she looked like the nymph of a wood-brook, a haunter of shadows, a creature sprung from the wild. But she was mortal maid, and he— what a fool he had been! Presently he would laugh at himself, when this dazed agony should clear away from his brain. He followed her down the long field to the bay shore. Now and then she paused and looked back to see if he were coming, but she never spoke. When she reached the shore road she turned and went along it until they came to an old grey house fronting the calm grey harbour. At its gate she paused. Roger knew now who she was. Catherine had told him about her a month ago.

She was Lilith Barr, a girl of eighteen, who had come to live with her uncle and aunt. Her father had died some months before. She was absolutely deaf as the result of some accident in childhood, and she was, as his own eyes told him, exquisitely lovely in her white, haunting style. But she was not Isabel Temple; he had tricked himself—he had lived in a fool's paradise—oh, he must get away and laugh at himself. He left her at her gate, disregarding the little hand she put timidly out—but he did not laugh at himself. He went back to Isabel Temple's grave and flung himself down on it and cried like a boy. He wept his stormy, anguished soul out on it; and when he rose and went away, he believed it was forever. He thought he could never, never go there again.

Catherine looked at him curiously the next morning. He looked wretched—haggard and hollow-eyed. She knew he had not come in till the summer dawn. But he had lost the rapt, uncanny look she hated; suddenly she no longer felt afraid of him. With this, she began to ask questions again.

"What kept ye out so late again last night, b'y?" she said reproachfully.

Roger looked at her in her morning ugliness. He had not really seen her for weeks. Now she smote on his tortured senses, so long drugged with beauty, like a physical blow. He suddenly burst into a laughter that frightened her.

"Preserve's, b'y, have ye gone mad? Or," she added, "have ye seen Isabel Temple's ghost?"

"No," said Roger loudly and explosively. "Don't talk any more about that damned ghost. Nobody ever saw it. The whole story is balderdash."

He got up and went violently out, leaving Catherine aghast. Was it possible Roger had sworn? What on earth had come over the b'y? But come what had or come what would, he no longer looked *fey*—there was that much to be thankful for. Even an occasional oath was better than that. Catherine went stiffly about her dish-washing, resolving to have 'Liza Adams to supper some night.

For a week Roger lived in agony—an agony of shame and humiliation and self-contempt. Then, when the edge of his bitter disappointment wore away, he made another dreadful discovery. He still loved her and longed for her just as keenly as before. He wanted madly to see her—her flower-like face, her great, ask-ing eyes, the sleek, braided flow of her hair. Ghost or woman—spirit or flesh—it mattered not. He could not live without her. At last his hunger for her drew him to the old grey house on the bay shore. He knew he was a fool—she would never look at him; he was only feeding the flame that must consume him. But go he must and did, seeking for his lost paradise.

He did not see her when he went in, but Mrs. Barr received him kindly and talked about her in a pleas-ant garrulous fashion which jarred on Roger, yet he listened greedily. Lilith, her aunt told him, had been made deaf by the accidental explosion of a gun when she was eight years old. She could not hear a sound but she could talk.

"A little, that is—not much, but enough to get along with. But she don't like talking somehow—dunno why. She's shy—and we think maybe she don't like to talk much because she can't hear her own voice. She don't ever speak except just when she has to. But she's been trained to lip-reading something wonderful—she can understand anything that's said when she can see the person that's talking. Still, it's a terrible drawback for the poor child—she's never had any real girl-life and she's dreadful sensitive and retiring. We can't get her to go out anywhere, only for lonely walks along shore by herself. We're much obliged for what you did the other night. It ain't safe for her to wander about alone as she does, but it ain't often anybody from the harbour gets up this far. She was dreadful upset about it—hasn't got over her scare yet."

When Lilith came in, her ivory-white face went scarlet all over at the sight of Roger. She sat down in a shadowy corner. Mrs. Barr got up and went out. Roger was mute; he could find nothing to say. He could have talked glibly enough to Isabel Temple's ghost in some unearthly tryst by her grave, but he could not find a word to say to this slip of flesh and blood. He felt very foolish and absurd, and very conscious of his twisted shoulder. What a fool he had been to come!

Then Lilith looked up at him—and smiled. A little shy, friendly smile. Roger suddenly saw her not as the tantalizing, unreal, mystic thing of the twilit grove, but as a little human creature, exquisitely pretty in her young-moon beauty, longing for companionship. He got up, forgetting his ugliness, and went across the room to her.

"Will you come for a walk," he said eagerly. He held out his hand like a child; as a child she stood up and took it; like two children they went out and down the sunset shore. Roger was again incredibly happy. It was not the same happiness as had been his in that vanished fortnight; it was a homelier happiness with its feet on the earth. The amazing thing was that he felt she was happy too—happy because she was walking with *him*, "Jarback" Temple, whom no girl had even thought about. A certain secret well-spring of fancy that had seemed dry welled up in him sparklingly again.

Through the summer weeks the odd courtship went on. Roger talked to her as he had never talked to anyone. He did not find it in the least hard to talk to her, though her necessity of watching his face so closely while he talked bothered him occasionally. He felt that her intent gaze was reading his soul as well as his lips. She never talked much herself; what she did say she spoke so low that it was hardly above a whisper, but she had a voice as lovely as her face—sweet, cadenced, haunting. Roger was quite mad about her, and he was horribly afraid that he could never get up enough courage to ask her to marry him. And he was afraid that if he did, she would never consent. In spite of her shy, eager welcomes he could not believe she could care for him—for *him*. She liked him, she was sorry for him, but it was unthinkable that she, white, exquisite Lilith, could marry him and sit at his table and his hearth. He was a fool to dream of it.

To the existence of romance and glamour in which he lived, no gossip of the countryside penetrated. Yet much gossip there was, and at last it came blundering in on Roger to destroy his fairy world a second time. He came downstairs one night in the twilight, ready to go to Lilith. His aunt and an old crony were talking in the kitchen; the crony was old, and Catherine, supposing Roger was out of the house, was talking loudly in that horrible voice of hers with still more horrible zest and satisfaction.

"Yes, I'm guessing it'll be a match as ye say. Oh the b'y's doing well. He ain't for every market, as I'm bound to admit. Ef she wan't deaf she wouldn't look at him, no doubt. But she has scads of money—they won't need to do a tap of work unless they like—and she's a good housekeeper too her aunt tells me. She's pretty enough to suit him—he's as particular as never was—and he wan't crooked and she wan't deaf when they was born, so it's likely their children will be all right. I'm that proud when I think of the match."

Roger fled out of the house, white of face and sick of heart. He went, not to the bay shore, but to Isabel Temple's grave. He had never been there since the night when he had rescued Lilith, but now he rushed to it in his new agony. His aunt's horrible practicalities had filled him with disgust—they dragged his love in the dust of sordid things. And Lilith was rich; he had never known that—never suspected it. He could never ask her to marry him now; he must never see her again. For the second time he had lost her, and this second losing could not be borne.

He sat down on the big boulder by the grave and dropped his poor grey face in his hands, moaning in anguish. Nothing was left him, not even dreams. He hoped he could soon die.

He did not know how long he sat there—he did not know when she came. But when he lifted his miserable eyes, he saw her, sitting just a little way from him on the big stone and looking at him with something in her face that made his heart beat madly. He forgot Aunt Catherine's sacrilege—he forgot that he was a presumptuous fool. He bent forward and kissed her lips for the first time. The wonder of it loosed his bound tongue.

"Lilith," he gasped, "I love you."

She put her hand into his and nestled closer to him.

"I thought you would have told me that long ago," she said.

The Girl and the Photograph

When I heard that Peter Austin was in Vancouver I hunted him up. I had met Peter ten years before when I had gone east to visit my father's people and had spent a few weeks with an uncle in Croyden. The Austins lived across the street from Uncle Tom, and Peter and I had struck up a friendship, although he was a hobbledehoy of awkward sixteen and I, at twenty-two, was older and wiser and more dignified than I've ever been since or ever expect to be again. Peter was a jolly little round freckled chap. He was all right when no girls were around; when they were he retired within himself like a misanthropic oyster, and was about as interesting. This was the one point upon which we always disagreed. Peter couldn't endure girls; I was devoted to them by the wholesale. The Croyden girls were pretty and vivacious. I had a score of flirtations during my brief sojourn among them.

But when I went away the face I carried in my memory was not that of any girl with whom I had walked and driven and played the game of hearts.

It was ten years ago, but I had never been quite able to forget that girl's face. Yet I had seen it but once and then only for a moment. I had gone for a solitary ramble in the woods over the river and, in a lonely little valley dim with pines, where I thought myself alone, I had come suddenly upon her, standing ankle-deep in fern on the bank of a brook, the late evening sunshine falling yellowly on her uncovered dark hair. She was very young—no more than sixteen; yet the face and eyes were already those of a woman. Such a face! Beautiful? Yes, but I thought of that afterward, when I was alone.

With that face before my eyes I thought only of its purity and sweetness, of the lovely soul and rich mind looking out of the great, greyish-blue eyes which, in the dimness of the pine shadows, looked almost black. There was something in the face of that child-woman I had never seen before and was destined never to see again in any other face. Careless boy though I was, it stirred me to the deeps. I felt that she must have been waiting forever in that pine valley for me and that, in finding her, I had found all of good that life could offer me.

I would have spoken to her, but before I could shape my greeting into words that should not seem rude or presumptuous, she had turned and gone, stepping lightly across the brook and vanishing in the maple copse beyond. For no more than ten seconds had I gazed into her face, and the soul of her, the real woman behind the fair outwardness, had looked back into my eyes; but I had never been able to forget it.

When I returned home I questioned my cousins diplomatically as to who she might be. I felt strangely reluctant to do so—it seemed in some way sacrilege; yet only by so doing could I hope to discover her. They could tell me nothing; nor did I meet her again during the remainder of my stay in Croyden, although I never went anywhere without looking for her, and haunted the pine valley daily, in the hope of seeing her again. My disappointment was so bitter that I laughed at myself.

I thought I was a fool to feel thus about a girl I had met for a moment in a chance ramble—a mere child at that, with her hair still hanging in its long glossy schoolgirl braid. But when I remembered her eyes, my wisdom forgave me.

Well, that was ten years ago; in those ten years the memory had, I must confess, grown dimmer. In our busy western life a man had not much time for sentimental recollections. Yet I had never been able to care for another woman. I wanted to; I wanted to marry and settle down. I had come to the time of life when a man wearies of drifting and begins to hanker for a calm anchorage in some snug haven of his own. But, somehow, I shirked the matter. It seemed rather easier to let things slide.

At this stage Peter came west. He was something in a bank, and was as round and jolly as ever; but he had evidently changed his attitude towards girls, for his rooms were full of their photos. They were stuck around everywhere and they were all pretty. Either Peter had excellent taste, or the Croyden photographers knew how to flatter. But there was one on the mantel which attracted my attention especially. If the photo were to be trusted the girl was quite the prettiest I had ever seen.

"Peter, what pretty girl's picture is this on your mantel?" I called out to Peter, who was in his bedroom, donning evening dress for some function.

"That's my cousin, Marian Lindsay," he answered. "She *is* rather nice-looking, isn't she. Lives in Croyden now—used to live up the river at Chiselhurst. Didn't you ever chance across her when you were in Croyden?"

"No," I said. "If I had I wouldn't have forgotten her face."

"Well, she'd be only a kid then, of course. She's twenty-six now. Marian is a mighty nice girl, but she's bound to be an old maid. She's got notions—ideals, she calls 'em. All the Croyden fellows have been in love with her at one time or another but they might as well have made up to a statue. Marian really hasn't a spark of feeling or sentiment in her. Her looks are the best part of her, although she's confoundedly clever."

Peter spoke rather squiffily. I suspected that he had been one of the smitten swains himself. I looked at the photo for a few minutes longer, admiring it more every minute and, when I heard Peter coming out, I did an unjustifiable thing—I took that photo and put it in my pocket.

I expected Peter would make a fuss when he missed it, but that very night the house in which he lived was burned to the ground. Peter escaped with the most important of his goods and chattels, but all the counterfeit presentments of his dear divinities went up in smoke. If he ever thought particularly of Marian Lindsay's photograph he must have supposed that it shared the fate of the others.

As for me, I propped my ill-gotten treasure up on my mantel and worshipped it for a fortnight. At the end of that time I went boldly to Peter and told him I wanted him to introduce me by letter to his dear cousin and ask her to agree to a friendly correspondence with me.

Oddly enough, I did not do this without some

reluctance, in spite of the fact that I was as much in love with Marian Lindsay as it was possible to be through the medium of a picture. I thought of the girl I had seen in the pine wood and felt an inward shrinking from a step that might divide me from her forever. But I rated myself for this nonsense. It was in the highest degree unlikely that I should ever meet the girl of the pines again. If she were still living she was probably some other man's wife. I would think no more about it.

Peter whistled when he heard what I had to say.

"Of course I'll do it, old man," he said obligingly. "But I warn you I don't think it will be much use. Marian isn't the sort of girl to open up a correspondence in such a fashion. However, I'll do the best I can for you."

"Do. Tell her I'm a respectable fellow with no violent bad habits and all that. I'm in earnest, Peter. I want to make that girl's acquaintance, and this seems the only way at present. I can't get off just now for a trip east. Explain all this, and use your cousinly influence in my behalf if you possess any."

Peter grinned.

"It's not the most graceful job in the world you are putting on me, Curtis," he said. "I don't mind owning up now that I was pretty far gone on Marian myself two years ago. It's all over now, but it was bad while it lasted. Perhaps Marian will consider your request more favourably if I put it in the light of a favour to myself. She must feel that she owes me something for wrecking my life."

Peter grinned again and looked at the one photo he had contrived to rescue from the fire. It was a pretty, snub-nosed little girl. She would never have consoled me for the loss of Marian Lindsay, but every man to his taste.

In due time Peter sought me out to give me his cousin's answer.

"Congratulations, Curtis. You've out-Caesared Caesar. You've conquered without even going and seeing. Marian agrees to a friendly correspondence with you. I am amazed, I admit—even though I did paint you up as a sort of Sir Galahad and Lancelot combined. I'm not used to seeing proud Marian do stunts like that, and it rather takes my breath."

I wrote to Marian Lindsay after one farewell dream

of the girl under the pines. When Marian's letters began to come regularly I forgot the other one altogether.

Such letters—such witty, sparkling, clever, womanly, delightful letters! They completed the conquest her picture had begun. Before we had corresponded six months I was besottedly in love with this woman whom I had never seen. Finally, I wrote and told her so, and I asked her to be my wife.

A fortnight later her answer came. She said frankly that she believed she had learned to care for me during our correspondence, but that she thought we should meet in person, before coming to any definite understanding. Could I not arrange to visit Croyden in the summer? Until then we would better continue on our present footing.

I agreed to this, but I considered myself practically engaged, with the personal meeting merely to be regarded as a sop to the Cerberus of conventionality. I permitted myself to use a decidedly lover-like tone in my letters henceforth, and I hailed it as a favourable omen that I was not rebuked for this, although Marian's own letters still retained their pleasant, simple friendliness.

Peter had at first tormented me mercilessly about the affair, but when he saw I did not like his chaff he stopped it. Peter was always a good fellow. He realized that I regarded the matter seriously, and he saw me off when I left for the east with a grin tempered by honest sympathy and understanding.

"Good luck to you," he said. "If you win Marian Lindsay you'll win a pearl among women. I haven't been able to grasp her taking to you in this fashion, though. It's so unlike Marian. But, since she undoubtedly has, you are a lucky man."

I arrived in Croyden at dusk and went to Uncle Tom's. There I found them busy with preparations for a party to be given that night in honour of a girl friend who was visiting my cousin Edna. I was secretly annoyed, for I wanted to hasten at once to Marian. But I couldn't decently get away, and on second thoughts I was consoled by the reflection that she would probably come to the party. I knew she belonged to the same social set as Uncle Tom's girls. I should, however, have preferred our meeting to have been under different circumstances.

From my stand behind the palms in a corner I

eagerly scanned the guests as they arrived. Suddenly my heart gave a bound. Marian Lindsay had just come in.

I recognized her at once from her photograph. It had not flattered her in the least; indeed, it had not done her justice, for her exquisite colouring of hair and complexion were quite lost in it. She was, moreover, gowned with a taste and smartness eminently admirable in the future Mrs. Eric Curtis. I felt a thrill of proprietary pride as I stepped out from behind the palms. She was talking to Aunt Grace; but her eyes fell on me. I expected a little start of recognition, for I had sent her an excellent photograph of myself; but her gaze was one of blankest unconsciousness.

I felt something like disappointment at her non-recognition, but I consoled myself by the reflection that people often fail to recognize other people whom they have seen only in photographs, no matter how good the likeness may be. I waylaid Edna, who was passing at that time, and said, "Edna I want you to introduce me to the girl who is talking to your mother."

Edna laughed.

"So you have succumbed at first sight to our

Croyden beauty? Of course I'll introduce you, but I warn you beforehand that she is the most incorrigible flirt in Croyden or out of it. So take care."

It jarred on me to hear Marian called a flirt. It seemed so out of keeping with her letters and the womanly delicacy and fineness revealed in them. But I reflected that women sometimes find it hard to forgive another woman who absorbs more than her share of lovers, and generally take their revenge by dubbing her a flirt, whether she deserves the name or not.

We had crossed the room during this reflection. Marian turned and stood before us, smiling at Edna, but evincing no recognition whatever of myself. It is a piquant experience to find yourself awaiting an introduction to a girl to whom you are virtually engaged.

"Dorothy dear," said Edna, "this is my cousin, Mr. Curtis, from Vancouver. Eric, this is Miss Armstrong."

I suppose I bowed. Habit carries us mechanically through many impossible situations. I don't know what I looked like or what I said, if I said anything. I don't suppose I betrayed my dire confusion, for Edna went off unconcernedly without another glance at me.

Dorothy Armstrong! Gracious powers—who—where—why? If this girl was Dorothy Armstrong who was Marian Lindsay? To whom was I engaged? There was some awful mistake somewhere, for it could not be possible that there were two girls in Croyden who looked exactly like the photograph reposing in my valise at that very moment. I stammered like a schoolboy.

"I—oh—I—your face seems familiar to me, Miss Armstrong. I—I—think I must have seen your photograph somewhere."

"Probably in Peter Austin's collection," smiled Miss Armstrong. "He had one of mine before he was burned out. How is he?"

"Peter? Oh, he's well," I replied vaguely. I was thinking a hundred words to the second, but my thoughts arrived nowhere. I was staring at Miss Armstrong like a man bewitched. She must have thought me a veritable booby. "Oh, by the way—can you tell me—do you know a Miss Lindsay in Croyden?"

Miss Armstrong looked surprised and a little bored. Evidently she was not used to having newly introduced young men inquiring about another girl.

"Marian Lindsay? Oh, yes."

"Is she here tonight?" I said.

"No, Marian is not going to parties just now, owing to the recent death of her aunt, who lived with them."

"Does she—oh—does she look like you at all?" I inquired idiotically.

Amusement glimmered but over Miss Armstrong's boredom. She probably concluded that I was some harmless lunatic.

"Like me? Not at all. There couldn't be two people more dissimilar. Marian is quite dark. I am fair. And our features are altogether unlike. Why, good evening, Jack. Yes, I believe I did promise you this dance."

She bowed to me and skimmed away with Jack. I saw Aunt Grace bearing down upon me and fled incontinently. In my own room I flung myself on a chair and tried to think the matter out. Where did the mistake come in? How had it happened? I shut my eyes and conjured up the vision of Peter's room that day. I remembered vaguely that, when I had picked up Dorothy Armstrong's picture, I had noticed another photograph that had fallen face downward beside it.

That must have been Marian Lindsay's, and Peter had thought I meant it.

And now what a position I was in! I was conscious of bitter disappointment. I had fallen in love with Dorothy Armstrong's photograph. As far as external semblance goes it was she whom I loved. I was practically engaged to another woman—a woman who, in spite of our correspondence, seemed to me now, in the shock of this discovery, a stranger. It was useless to tell myself that it was the mind and soul revealed in those letters that I loved, and that that mind and soul were Marian Lindsay's. It was useless to remember that Peter had said she was pretty. Exteriorly, she was a stranger to me; hers was not the face which had risen before me for nearly a year as the face of the woman I loved. Was ever unlucky wretch in such a predicament before?

Well, there was only one thing to do. I must stand by my word. Marian Lindsay was the woman I had asked to marry me, whose answer I must shortly go to receive. If that answer were "yes" I must accept the situation and banish all thought of Dorothy Armstrong's pretty face.

Next evening at sunset I went to "Glenwood," the

Lindsay place. Doubtless, an eager lover might have gone earlier, but an eager lover I certainly was not. Probably Marian was expecting me and had given orders concerning me, for the maid who came to the door conveyed me to a little room behind the stairs—a room which, as I felt as soon as I entered it, was a woman's pet domain. In its books and pictures and flowers it spoke eloquently of dainty femininity. Somehow, it suited the letters. I did not feel quite so much the stranger as I had felt. Nevertheless, when I heard a light footfall on the stairs my heart beat painfully. I stood up and turned to the door, but I could not look up. The footsteps came nearer; I knew that a white hand swept aside the *portière* at the entrance; I knew that she had entered the room and was standing before me.

With an effort I raised my eyes and looked at her. She stood, tall and gracious, in a ruby splendour of sunset falling through the window beside her. The light quivered like living radiance over a dark proud head, a white throat, and a face before whose perfect loveliness the memory of Dorothy Armstrong's laughing prettiness faded like a star in the sunrise, nevermore in the fullness of the day to be remembered. Yet it was not of her beauty I thought as I stood spellbound before her. I seemed to see a dim little valley full of whispering pines, and a girl standing under their shadows, looking at me with the same great, greyish-blue eyes which gazed upon me now from Marian Lindsay's face—the same face, matured into gracious womanhood, that I had seen ten years ago; and loved—aye, loved—ever since. I took an unsteady step forward.

"Marian?" I said.

When I got home that night I burned Dorothy Armstrong's photograph. The next day I went to my cousin Tom, who owns the fashionable studio of Croyden and, binding him over to secrecy, sought one of Marian's latest photographs from him. It is the only secret I have ever kept from my wife.

Before we were married Marian told me something.

"I always remembered you as you looked that day under the pines," she said. "I was only a child, but I think I loved you then and ever afterwards. When I dreamed my girl's dream of love your face rose up before me. I had the advantage of you that I knew your name—I had heard of you. When Peter wrote about you I knew who you were. That was why I agreed to correspond with you. I was afraid it was a forward—an unwomanly thing to do. But it seemed my chance for happiness and I took it. I am glad I did."

I did not answer in words, but lovers will know how I did answer.

The Gossip of Valley View

It was the first of April, and Julius Barrett, aged fourteen, perched on his father's gatepost, watched ruefully the low descending sun, and counted that day lost. He had not succeeded in "fooling" a single person, although he had tried repeatedly. One and all, old and young, of his intended victims had been too wary for Julius. Hence, Julius was disgusted and ready for anything in the way of a stratagem or a spoil.

The Barrett gatepost topped the highest hill in Valley View. Julius could see the entire settlement, from "Young" Thomas Everett's farm, a mile to the west, to

Adelia Williams's weather-grey little house on a moon-rise slope to the east. He was gazing moodily down the muddy road when Dan Chester, homeward bound from the post office, came riding sloppily along on his grey mare and pulled up by the Barrett gate to hand a paper to Julius.

Dan was a young man who took life and himself very seriously. He seldom smiled, never joked, and had a Washingtonian reputation for veracity. Dan had never told a conscious falsehood in his life; he never even exaggerated.

Julius, beholding Dan's solemn face, was seized with a perfectly irresistible desire to "fool" him. At the same moment his eye caught the dazzling reflection of the setting sun on the windows of Adelia Williams's house, and he had an inspiration little short of diaboli-cal. "Have you heard the news, Dan?" he asked.

"No, what is it?" asked Dan.

"I dunno's I ought to tell it," said Julius reflectively. "It's kind of a family affair, but then Adelia didn't say not to, and anyway it'll be all over the place soon. So I'll tell you, Dan, if you'll promise never to tell who told you. Adelia Williams and Young Thomas Everett are going to be married."

Julius delivered himself of this tremendous lie with a transparently earnest countenance. Yet Dan, credulous as he was, could not believe it all at once.

"Git out," he said.

"It's true, 'pon my word," protested Julius. "Adelia was up last night and told Ma all about it. Ma's her cousin, you know. The wedding is to be in June, and Adelia asked Ma to help her get her quilts and things ready."

Julius reeled all this off so glibly that Dan finally believed the story, despite the fact that the people thus coupled together in prospective matrimony were the very last people in Valley View who could have been expected to marry each other. Young Thomas was a confirmed bachelor of fifty, and Adelia Williams was forty; they were not supposed to be even well acquainted, as the Everetts and the Williamses had never been very friendly, although no open feud existed between them.

Nevertheless, in view of Julius's circumstantial statements, the amazing news must be true, and Dan was instantly agog to carry it further. Julius watched Dan and the grey mare out of sight, fairly writhing with ecstasy. Oh, but Dan had been easy! The story would be all over Valley View in twenty-four hours. Julius laughed until he came near to falling off the gatepost.

At this point Julius and Danny drop out of our story, and Young Thomas enters.

It was two days later when Young Thomas heard that he was to be married to Adelia Williams in June. Eben Clark, the blacksmith, told him when he went to the forge to get his horse shod. Young Thomas laughed his big jolly laugh. Valley View gossip had been marrying him off for the last thirty years, although never before to Adelia Williams.

"It's news to me," he said tolerantly.

Eben grinned broadly. "Ah, you can't bluff it off like that, Tom," he said. "The news came too straight this time. Well, I was glad to hear it, although I was mighty surprised. I never thought of you and Adelia. But she's a fine little woman and will make you a capital wife."

Young Thomas grunted and drove away. He had a good deal of business to do that day, involving calls at various places—the store for molasses, the mill for flour, Jim Bentley's for seed grain, the doctor's for toothache drops for his housekeeper, the post office for mail—and at each and every place he was joked about his approaching marriage. In the end it rather annoyed Young Thomas. He drove home at last in what was for him something of a temper. How on earth had that fool story started? With such detailed circumstantiality of rugs and quilts, too? Adelia Williams must be going to marry somebody, and the Valley View gossips, unable to locate the man, had guessed Young Thomas.

When he reached home, tired, mud-bespattered, and hungry, his housekeeper, who was also his hired man's wife, asked him if it was true that he was going to be married. Young Thomas, taking in at a glance the ill-prepared, half-cold supper on the table, felt more annoyed than ever, and said it wasn't, with a strong expression—not quite an oath—for Young Thomas never swore, unless swearing be as much a matter of intonation as of words.

Mrs. Dunn sighed, patted her swelled face, and said she was sorry; she had hoped it was true, for her man had decided to go west. They were to go in a month's time. Young Thomas sat down to his supper with the prospect of having to look up another housekeeper and hired man before planting to destroy his appetite.

Next day, three people who came to see Young Thomas on business congratulated him on his approaching marriage. Young Thomas, who had recovered his usual good humour, merely laughed. There was no use in being too earnest in denial, he thought. He knew that his unusual fit of petulance with his housekeeper had only convinced her that the story was true. It would die away in time, as other similar stories had died, he thought. Valley View gossip was imaginative.

Young Thomas looked rather serious, however, when the minister and his wife called that evening and referred to the report. Young Thomas gravely said that it was unfounded. The minister looked graver still and said he was sorry—he had hoped it was true. His wife glanced significantly about Young Thomas's big, untidy sitting-room, where there were cobwebs on the ceiling and fluff in the corners and dust on the mop-board, and said nothing, but looked volumes.

"Dang it all," said Young Thomas, as they drove away, "they'll marry me yet in spite of myself."

The gossip made him think about Adelia Williams. He had never thought about her before; he was barely acquainted with her. Now he remembered that she was a plump, jolly-looking little woman, noted for being a good housekeeper. Then Young Thomas groaned, remembering that he must start out looking for a housekeeper soon; and housekeepers were not easily found, as Young Thomas had discovered several times since his mother's death ten years before.

Next Sunday in church Young Thomas looked at Adelia Williams. He caught Adelia looking at him. Adelia blushed and looked guiltily away.

"Dang it all," reflected Young Thomas, forgetting that he was in church. "I suppose she has heard that fool story too. I'd like to know the person who started it; man or woman, I'd punch their head."

Nevertheless, Young Thomas went on looking at Adelia by fits and starts, although he did not again catch Adelia looking at him. He noticed that she had round rosy cheeks and twinkling brown eyes. She did not look like an old maid, and Young Thomas wondered that she had been allowed to become one. Sarah Barnett, now, to whom report had married him a year ago, looked like a dried sour apple.

For the next four weeks the story haunted Young Thomas like a spectre. Down it would not. Everywhere he went he was joked about it. It gathered fresh detail every week. Adelia was getting her clothes ready; she was to be married in seal-brown cashmere; Vinnie Lawrence at Valley Centre was making it for her; she had got a new hat with a long ostrich plume; some said white, some said grey.

Young Thomas kept wondering who the man could be, for he was convinced that Adelia was going to marry somebody. More than that, once he caught himself wondering enviously. Adelia was a nice-looking woman, and he had not so far heard of any probable housekeeper.

"Dang it all," said Young Thomas to himself in desperation. "I wouldn't care if it was true."

His married sister from Carlisle heard the story and came over to investigate. Young Thomas denied it shortly, and his sister scolded. She had devoutly hoped it was true, she said, and it would have been a great weight off her mind.

"This house is in a disgraceful condition, Thomas," she said severely. "It would break Mother's heart if she could rise out of her grave to see it. And Adelia Williams is a perfect housekeeper."

"You didn't use to think so much of the Williams crowd," said Young Thomas drily.

"Oh, some of them don't amount to much," admitted Maria, "but Adelia is all right."

Catching sight of an odd look on Young Thomas's face, she added hastily, "Thomas Everett, I believe it's true after all. Now, is it? For mercy's sake don't be so sly. You might tell me, your own and only sister, if it is."

"Oh, shut up," was Young Thomas's unfeeling reply to his own and only sister.

Young Thomas told himself that night that Valley View gossip would drive him into an asylum yet if it didn't let up. He also wondered if Adelia was as much persecuted as himself. No doubt she was. He never could catch her eye in church now, but he would have been surprised had he realized how many times he tried to.

The climax came the third week in May, when Young Thomas, who had been keeping house for himself for three weeks, received a letter and an express box from his cousin, Charles Everett, out in Manitoba. Charles and he had been chums in their boyhood. They corresponded occasionally still, although it was twenty years since Charles had gone west.

The letter was to congratulate Young Thomas on his approaching marriage. Charles had heard of it through some Valley View correspondents of his wife. He was much pleased; he had always liked Adelia, he said—had been an old beau of hers, in fact. Thomas might give her a kiss for him if he liked. He forwarded a wedding present by express and hoped they would be very happy, etc.

The present was an elaborate hatrack of polished buffalo horns, mounted on red plush, with an inset mirror. Young Thomas set it up on the kitchen table and scowled moodily at his reflection in the mirror. If wedding presents were beginning to come, it was high time something was done. The matter was past being a joke. This affair of the present would certainly get out— things always got out in Valley View, dang it all—and he would never hear the last of it.

"I'll marry," said Young Thomas decisively. "If Adelia Williams won't have me, I'll marry the first woman who will, if it's Sarah Barnett herself."

Young Thomas shaved and put on his Sunday suit. As soon as it was safely dark, he hied him away to Adelia Williams. He felt very doubtful about his reception, but the remembrance of the twinkle in Adelia's brown eyes comforted him. She looked like a woman who had a sense of humour; she might not take him, but she would not feel offended or insulted because he asked her.

"Dang it all, though, I hope she will take me," said Young Thomas. "I'm in for getting married now and no mistake. And I can't get Adelia out of my head. I've been thinking of her steady ever since that confounded gossip began."

When he knocked at Adelia's door he discovered that his face was wet with perspiration. Adelia opened the door and started when she saw him; then she turned very red and stiffly asked him in. Young Thomas went in and sat down, wondering if all men felt so horribly uncomfortable when they went courting.

Adelia stooped low over the woodbox to put a stick of wood in the stove, for the May evening was chilly. Her shoulders were shaking; the shaking grew worse; suddenly Adelia laughed hysterically and, sitting down on the woodbox, continued to laugh. Young Thomas eyed her with a friendly grin.

"Oh, do excuse me," gasped poor Adelia, wiping tears from her eyes. "This is—dreadful—I didn't mean to laugh—I don't know why I'm laughing—but—I—can't help it."

She laughed helplessly again. Young Thomas laughed too. His embarrassment vanished in the mellowness of that laughter. Presently Adelia composed herself and removed from the woodbox to a chair, but there was still a suspicious twitching about the corners of her mouth.

"I suppose," said Young Thomas, determined to have it over with before the ice could form again, "I suppose, Adelia, you've heard the story that's been going about you and me of late?"

Adelia nodded. "I've been persecuted to the verge of insanity with it," she said. "Every soul I've seen has tormented me about it, and people have written me about it. I've denied it till I was black in the face, but nobody believed me. I can't find out how it started. I hope you believe, Mr. Everett, that it couldn't possibly have arisen from anything I said. I've felt dreadfully worried for fear you might think it did. I heard that my cousin, Lucilla Barrett, said I told her, but Lucilla vowed to me that she never said such a thing or even dreamed of it. I've felt dreadful bad over the whole affair. I even gave up the idea of making a quilt after a lovely new pattern I've got because they made such a talk about my brown dress."

"I've been kind of supposing that you must be going to marry somebody, and folks just guessed it was me," said Young Thomas—he said it anxiously.

"No, I'm not going to be married to anybody," said Adelia with a laugh, taking up her knitting.

"I'm glad of that," said Young Thomas gravely. "I mean," he hastened to add, seeing the look of astonishment on Adelia's face, "that I'm glad there isn't any other man because—because I want you myself, Adelia."

Adelia laid down her knitting and blushed crimson. But she looked at Young Thomas squarely and reproachfully.

"You needn't think you are bound to say that because of the gossip, Mr. Everett," she said quietly.

"Oh, I don't," said Young Thomas earnestly. "But the truth is, the story set me to thinking about you, and from that I got to wishing it was true—honest, I did—I couldn't get you out of my head, and at last I didn't want to. It just seemed to me that you were the very woman for me if you'd only take me. Will you, Adelia? I've got a good farm and house, and I'll try to make you happy."

It was not a very romantic wooing, perhaps. But Adelia was forty and had never been a romantic little body even in the heyday of youth. She was a practical woman, and Young Thomas was a fine looking man of his age with abundance of worldly goods. Besides, she liked him, and the gossip had made her think a good deal about him of late. Indeed, in a moment of candour she had owned to herself the very last Sunday in church that she wouldn't mind if the story were true.

"I'll—I'll think of it," she said.

This was practically an acceptance, and Young Thomas so understood it. Without loss of time he crossed the kitchen, sat down beside Adelia, and put his arms about her plump waist.

"Here's a kiss Charlie sent me to give you," he said, giving it.

The Brothers Grimm

1785–1863, 1786–1859

The Raven

There was once a queen who had a little daughter, still too young to run alone. One day the child was very troublesome, and the mother could not quiet it, do what she would. She grew impatient, and seeing the ravens flying round the castle, she opened the window, and said: "I wish you were a raven and would fly away, then I should have a little peace." Scarcely were the words out of her mouth, when the child in her arms was turned into a raven, and flew away from her through the open window. The bird took its flight to a dark wood and remained there for a long time, and meanwhile the parents could hear nothing of their child.

Long after this, a man was making his way through the wood when he heard a raven calling, and he followed the sound of the voice. As he drew near, the raven said, "I am by birth a king's daughter, but am now under the spell of some enchantment; you can, however, set me free."

"What am I to do?" he asked.

She replied, "Go farther into the wood until you come to a house, wherein lives an old woman; she will offer you food and drink, but you must not take of either; if you do, you will fall into a deep sleep, and will not be able to help me. In the garden behind the house is a large tan-heap, and on that you must stand and watch for me. I shall drive there in my carriage at two o'clock in the afternoon for three successive days; the first day it will be drawn by four white, the second by four chestnut, and the last by four black horses; but if you fail to keep awake and I find you sleeping, I shall not be set free."

The man promised to do all that she wished, but

the raven said, "Alas! I know even now that you will take something from the woman and be unable to save me." The man assured her again that he would on no account touch a thing to eat or drink.

When he came to the house and went inside, the old woman met him, and said, "Poor man! How tired you are! Come in and rest and let me give you something to eat and drink."

"No," answered the man, "I will neither eat not drink."

But she would not leave him alone, and urged him saying, "If you will not eat anything, at least you might take a draught of wine; one drink counts for nothing," and at last he allowed himself to be persuaded, and drank.

As it drew towards the appointed hour, he went outside into the garden and mounted the tan-heap to await the raven. Suddenly a feeling of fatigue came over him, and unable to resist it, he lay down for a little while, fully determined, however, to keep awake; but in another minute his eyes closed of their own accord, and he fell into such a deep sleep, that all the noises in the world would not have awakened him. At two o'clock the raven came driving along, drawn by her four white horses; but even before she reached the spot, she said to herself, sighing, "I know he has fallen asleep." When she entered the garden, there she found him as she had feared, lying on the tan-heap, fast asleep. She got out of her carriage and went to him; she called him and shook him, but it was all in vain, he still continued sleeping.

The next day at noon, the old woman came to him again with food and drink which he at first refused. At last, overcome by her persistent entreaties that he would take something, he lifted the glass and drank again.

Towards two o'clock he went into the garden and on to the tan-heap to watch for the raven. He had not been there long before he began to feel so tired that his limbs seemed hardly able to support him, and he could not stand upright any longer; so again he lay down and fell fast asleep. As the raven drove along her four chestnut horses, she said sorrowfully to herself, "I know he has fallen asleep." She went as before to look for him, but he slept, and it was impossible to awaken him.

The following day the old woman said to him, "What is this? You are not eating or drinking anything, do you want to kill yourself?'"

He answered, "I may not and will not either eat or drink."

But she put down the dish of food and the glass of wine in front of him, and when he smelt the wine, he was unable to resist the temptation, and took a deep draught.

When the hour came round again he went as usual on to the tan-heap in the garden to await the king's daughter, but he felt even more overcome with weariness than on the two previous days, and throwing himself down, he slept like a log. At two o'clock the raven could be seen approaching, and this time her coachman and everything about her, as well as her horses, were black.

She was sadder than ever as she drove along, and said mournfully, "I know he has fallen asleep, and will not be able to set me free." She found him sleeping heavily, and all her efforts to awaken him were of no avail. Then she placed beside him a loaf, and some meat, and a flask of wine, of such a kind, that however much he took of them, they would never grow less. After that she drew a gold ring, on which her name was engraved, off her finger, and put it upon one of his. Finally, she laid a letter near him, in which, after giving him particulars of the food and drink she had left for him, she finished with the following words: "I see that as long as you remain here you will never be able to set me free; if, however, you still wish to do so, come to the golden castle of Stromberg; this is well within your power to accomplish." She then returned to her carriage and drove to the golden castle of Stromberg.

When the man awoke and found that he had been sleeping, he was grieved at heart, and said, "She has no doubt been here and driven away again, and it is now too late for me to save her." Then his eyes fell on the things which were lying beside him; he read the letter, and knew from it all that had happened. He rose up without delay, eager to start on his way and to reach the castle of Stromberg, but he had no idea in which direction he ought to go. He travelled about a long time in search of it and came at last to a dark forest, through which he went on walking for fourteen days and still could not find a way out. Once more the night came on, and worn out he lay down under a bush and fell asleep. Again the next day he pursued his way through the forest, and that evening, thinking to rest again, he lay down as before, but he heard such a howling and wailing that he found it impossible to sleep. He waited till it was darker and people had begun to light up their houses, and then seeing a little glimmer ahead of him, he went towards it.

He found that the light came from a house which looked smaller than it really was, from the contrast of its height with that of an immense giant who stood in front of it. He thought to himself, "If the giant sees me going in, my life will not be worth much." However, after a while he summoned up courage and went forward.

When the giant saw him, he called out, "It is lucky for that you have come, for I have not had anything to eat for a long time. I can have you now for my supper."

"I would rather you let that alone," said the man, "for I do not willingly give myself up to be eaten; if you are wanting food I have enough to satisfy your hunger."

"If that is so," replied the giant, "I will leave you

in peace; I only thought of eating you because I had nothing else."

So they went indoors together and sat down, and the man brought out the bread, meat, and wine, which although he had eaten and drunk of them, were still unconsumed. The giant was pleased with the good cheer, and ate and drank to his heart's content. When he had finished his supper the man asked him if he could direct him to the castle of Stromberg. The giant said, "I will look on my map; on it are marked all the towns, villages, and houses." So he fetched his map, and looked for the castle, but could not find it. "Never mind," he said, "I have larger maps upstairs in the cupboard, we will look on those," but they searched in vain, for the castle was not marked even on these. The man now thought he should like to continue his journey, but the giant begged him to remain for a day or two longer until the return of his brother, who was away in search of provisions. When the brother came home, they asked him about the castle of Stromberg, and he told them he would look on his own maps as soon as he had eaten and appeased his hunger. Accordingly, when he had finished his supper, they all went up together to his room and looked through his maps, but the castle was not to be found. Then he fetched other older maps, and they went on looking for the castle until at last they found it, but it was many thousand miles away.

"How shall I be able to get there?" asked the man.

"I have two hours to spare," said the giant, "and I will carry you into the neighbourhood of the castle; I must then return to look after the child who is in our care."

The giant, thereupon, carried the man to within about a hundred leagues of the castle, where he left him, saying, "You will be able to walk the remainder of the way yourself." The man journeyed on day and night till he reached the golden castle of Stromberg. He found it situated, however, on a glass mountain, and looking up from the foot he saw the enchanted maiden drive round her castle and then go inside. He was overjoyed to see her, and longed to get to the top of the mountain, but the sides were so slippery that every time he attempted to climb he fell back again. When he saw that it was impossible to reach her, he was greatly grieved, and said to himself, "I will remain here and wait for her," so he built himself a little hut, and there he sat and watched for a whole year, and every day he saw the king's daughter driving round her castle, but still was unable to get nearer to her.

Looking out from his hut one day he saw three robbers fighting and he called out to them, "God be with you." They stopped when they heard the call, but looking round and seeing nobody, they went on again with their fighting, which now became more furious. "God be with you," he cried again, and again they paused and looked about, but seeing no one went back to their fighting. A third time he called out, "God be with you," and then thinking he should like to know the cause of dispute between the three men, he went out and asked them why they were fighting so angrily with one another. One of them said that he had found a stick, and that he had but to strike it against any door through which he wished to pass, and it immediately flew open. Another told him that he had found a cloak which rendered its wearer invisible; and the third had caught a horse which would carry its rider over any obstacle, and even up the glass mountain. They had been unable to decide whether they would keep together and have the things in common, or whether they would separate. On hearing this, the man said, "I will give you something in exchange for those three things; not money, for that I have not got, but something that is of far more value. I must first, however, prove whether all you have told me about your three things is true." The robbers, therefore, made him get on the horse, and handed him the stick and the cloak, and when he had put this round him he was no longer visible. Then he fell upon them with the stick and beat them one after another, crying, "There, you idle vagabonds, you have got what you deserve; are you satisfied now!"

After this he rode up the glass mountain. When he reached the gate of the castle, he found it closed, but he gave it a blow with his stick, and it flew wide open at once and he passed through. He mounted the steps and entered the room where the maiden was sitting, with a golden goblet full of wine in front of her. She could not see him for he still wore his cloak. He took the ring which she had given him off his finger, and threw it into the goblet, so that it rang as it touched the bottom. "That is my own ring," she exclaimed, "and if that is so the man must also be here who is coming to set me free."

She sought for him about the castle, but could find him nowhere. Meanwhile he had gone outside again and mounted his horse and thrown off the cloak. When therefore she came to the castle gate she saw him, and cried aloud for joy. Then he dismounted and took her in his arms; and she kissed him, and said, "Now you have indeed set me free, and tomorrow we will celebrate our marriage."

The Water of Life

Long before you or I were born, there reigned, in a country a great way off, a king who had three sons. This king once fell very ill—so ill that nobody thought he could live. His sons were very much grieved at their father's sickness; and as they were walking together very mournfully in the garden of the palace, a little old man met them and asked what was the matter. They told him that their father was very ill, and that they were afraid nothing could save him. "I know what would," said the little old man; "it is the Water of Life.

If he could have a draught of it he would be well again; but it is very hard to get."

Then the eldest son said, "I will soon find it": and he went to the sick king, and begged that he might go in search of the Water of Life, as it was the only thing that could save him.

"No," said the king. "I had rather die than place you in such great danger as you must meet with in your journey." But he begged so hard that the king let him go; and the prince thought to himself, "If I bring my father this water, he will make me sole heir to his kingdom."

Then he set out: and when he had gone on his way some time he came to a deep valley, overhung with rocks and woods; and as he looked around, he saw standing above him on one of the rocks a little ugly dwarf, with a sugarloaf cap and a scarlet cloak; and the dwarf called to him and said, "Prince, whither so fast?"

"What is that to thee, you ugly imp?" said the prince haughtily, and rode on.

But the dwarf was enraged at his behaviour, and laid a fairy spell of ill-luck upon him; so that as he rode on the mountain pass became narrower and narrower, and at last the way was so straitened that he could not go to step forward: and when he thought to have turned his horse round and go back the way he came, he heard a loud laugh ringing round him, and found that the path was closed behind him, so that he was shut in all round. He next tried to get off his horse and make his way on foot, but again the laugh rang in his ears, and he found himself unable to move a step, and thus he was forced to abide spellbound.

Meantime the old king was lingering on in daily hope of his son's return, till at last the second son said, "Father, I will go in search of the Water of Life." For he thought to himself, "My brother is surely dead, and the kingdom will fall to me if I find the water."

The king was at first very unwilling to let him go, but at last yielded to his wish. So he set out and followed the same road which his brother had done, and met with the same elf, who stopped him at the same spot in the mountains, saying, as before, "Prince, prince, whither so fast?"

"Mind your own affairs, busybody!" said the prince scornfully, and rode on.

But the dwarf put the same spell upon him as he put on his elder brother, and he, too, was at last obliged to take up his abode in the heart of the mountains. Thus it is with proud silly people, who think themselves above everyone else, and are too proud to ask or take advice.

When the second prince had thus been gone a long time, the youngest son said he would go and search for the Water of Life, and trusted he should soon be able to make his father well again. So he set out, and the dwarf met him too at the same spot in the valley, among the mountains, and said, "Prince, whither so fast?"

And the prince said, "I am going in search of the Water of Life, because my father is ill, and like to die: can you help me? Pray be kind, and aid me if you can!"

"Do you know where it is to be found?" asked the dwarf.

"No," said the prince, "I do not. Pray tell me if you know."

"Then as you have spoken to me kindly, and are wise enough to seek for advice, I will tell you how and where to go. The water you seek springs from a well in an enchanted castle; and, that you may be able to reach it in safety, I will give you an iron wand and two little loaves of bread; strike the iron door of the castle three times with the wand, and it will open: two hungry lions will be lying down inside gaping for their prey, but if you throw them the bread they will let you pass; then hasten on to the well, and take some of the Water of Life before the clock strikes twelve; for if you tarry longer the door will shut upon you for ever."

Then the prince thanked his little friend with the scarlet cloak for his friendly aid, and took the wand and the bread, and went travelling on and on, over sea and over land, till he came to his journey's end, and found everything to be as the dwarf had told him. The door flew open at the third stroke of the wand, and when the lions were quieted he went on through the castle and came at length to a beautiful hall. Around it he saw several knights sitting in a trance; then he pulled off their rings and put them on his own fingers. In another room he saw on a table a sword and a loaf of bread, which he also took. Further on he came to a room where a beautiful young lady sat upon a couch; and she welcomed him joyfully, and said, if he would set her free from the spell that bound her, the kingdom should be his, if he would come back in a year and marry her. Then she told him that the well that held the Water of Life was in the palace gardens; and bade him make haste, and draw what he wanted before the clock struck twelve.

He walked on; and as he walked through beautiful gardens he came to a delightful shady spot in which stood a couch; and he thought to himself, as he felt tired, that he would rest himself for a while, and gaze on the lovely scenes around him. So he laid himself down, and sleep fell upon him unawares, so that he did not wake up till the clock was striking a quarter to twelve. Then he sprang from the couch dreadfully frightened, ran to the well, filled a cup that was standing by him full of water, and hastened to get away in time. Just as he was going out of the iron door it struck twelve, and the door fell so quickly upon him that it snapped off a piece of his heel.

When he found himself safe, he was overjoyed to think that he had got the Water of Life; and as he was going on his way homewards, he passed by the little dwarf, who, when he saw the sword and the loaf, said,

"You have made a noble prize; with the sword you can at a blow slay whole armies, and the bread will never fail you."

Then the prince thought to himself, "I cannot go home to my father without my brothers"; so he said, "My dear friend, cannot you tell me where my two brothers are, who set out in search of the Water of Life before me, and never came back?"

"I have shut them up by a charm between two mountains," said the dwarf, "because they were proud and ill-behaved, and scorned to ask advice." The prince begged so hard for his brothers, that the dwarf at last set them free, though unwillingly, saying, "Beware of them, for they have bad hearts." Their brother, however, was greatly rejoiced to see them, and told them all that had happened to him; how he had found the Water of Life, and had taken a cup full of it; and how he had set a beautiful princess free from a spell that bound her; and how she had engaged to wait a whole year, and then to marry him, and to give him the kingdom.

Then they all three rode on together, and on their way home came to a country that was laid waste by war and a dreadful famine, so that it was feared all must die for want. But the prince gave the king of the land the bread, and all his kingdom ate of it. And he lent the king the wonderful sword, and he slew the enemy's army with it; and thus the kingdom was once more in peace and plenty. In the same manner he befriended two other countries through which they passed on their way.

When they came to the sea, they got into a ship and during their voyage the two eldest said to themselves, "Our brother has got the water which we could not find, therefore our father will forsake us and give him the kingdom, which is our right"; so they were full of envy and revenge, and agreed together how they could ruin him. Then they waited till he was fast asleep, and poured the Water of Life out of the cup, and took it for themselves, giving him bitter sea-water instead.

When they came to their journey's end, the youngest son brought his cup to the sick king, that he might drink and be healed. Scarcely, however, had he tasted the bitter sea-water when he became worse even than he was before; and then both the elder sons came in, and blamed the youngest for what they had done; and said that he wanted to poison their father, but that they had found the Water of Life, and had brought it with them. He no sooner began to drink of what they brought him, than he felt his sickness leave him, and was as strong and well as in his younger days. Then they went to their brother, and laughed at him, and said, "Well, brother, you found the Water of Life, did you? You have had the trouble and we shall have the reward. Pray, with all your cleverness, why did not you manage to keep your eyes open? Next year one of us will take away your beautiful princess, if you do not take care. You had better say nothing about this to our father, for he does not believe a word you say; and if you tell tales, you shall lose your life into the bargain: but be quiet, and we will let you off."

The old king was still very angry with his youngest son, and thought that he really meant to have taken away his life; so he called his court together, and asked what should be done, and all agreed that he ought to be put to death. The prince knew nothing of what was going on, till one day, when the king's chief huntsmen went a-hunting with him, and they were alone in the wood together, the huntsman looked so sorrowful that the prince said, "My friend, what is the matter with you?"

"I cannot and dare not tell you," said he.

But the prince begged very hard, and said, "Only tell me what it is, and do not think I shall be angry, for I will forgive you."

"Alas!" said the huntsman; "the king has ordered me to shoot you."

The prince started at this, and said, "Let me live, and I will change dresses with you; you shall take my royal coat to show to my father, and do you give me your shabby one."

"With all my heart," said the huntsman; "I am sure I shall be glad to save you, for I could not have shot you." Then he took the prince's coat, and gave him the shabby one, and went away through the wood.

Some time after, three grand embassies came to the old king's court, with rich gifts of gold and precious stones for his youngest son; now all these were sent from the three kings to whom he had lent his sword and loaf of bread, in order to rid them of their enemy and feed their people. This touched the old king's heart, and he thought his son might still be guiltless, and said to his court, "O that my son were still alive! How it grieves me that I had him killed!"

"He is still alive," said the huntsman; "and I am glad that I had pity on him, but let him go in peace, and brought home his royal coat." At this the king was overwhelmed with joy, and made it known throughout all his kingdom, that if his son would come back to his court he would forgive him.

Meanwhile the princess was eagerly waiting till her deliverer should come back; and had a road made leading up to her palace all of shining gold; and told her courtiers that whoever came on horseback, and rode straight up to the gate upon it, was her true lover; and that they must let him in: but whoever rode on one side of it, they must be sure was not the right one; and that they must send him away at once.

The time soon came, when the eldest brother thought that he would make haste to go to the princess, and say that he was the one who had set her free, and that he should have her for his wife, and the kingdom with her. As he came before the palace and saw the golden road, he stopped to look at it, and he thought to himself, "It is a pity to ride upon this beautiful road"; so he turned aside and rode on the right-hand side of it. But when he came to the gate, the guards, who had seen the road he took, said to him, he could not be what he said he was, and must go about his business.

The second prince set out soon afterwards on the same errand; and when he came to the golden road, and his horse had set one foot upon it, he stopped to look at it, and thought it very beautiful, and said to himself, "What a pity it is that anything should tread here!" Then he too turned aside and rode on the left side of it. But when he came to the gate the guards said he was not the true prince, and that he too must go away about his business; and away he went.

Now when the full year was come round, the third brother left the forest in which he had lain hid for fear of his father's anger, and set out in search of his betrothed bride. So he journeyed on, thinking of her all the way, and rode so quickly that he did not even see what the road was made of, but went with his horse straight over it; and as he came to the gate it flew open, and the princess welcomed him with joy, and said he was her deliverer, and should now be her husband and lord of the kingdom. When the first joy at their meeting was over, the princess told him she had heard of his father having forgiven him, and of his wish to have him home again: so, before his wedding with the princess, he went to visit his father, taking her with him. Then he told him everything; how his brothers had cheated and robbed him, and yet that he had borne all those wrongs for the love of his father. And the old king was very angry, and wanted to punish his wicked sons; but they made their escape, and got into a ship and sailed away over the wide sea, and where they went to nobody knew and nobody cared.

And now the old king gathered together his court, and asked all his kingdom to come and celebrate the wedding of his son and the princess. And young and old, noble and squire, gentle and simple, came at once on the summons; and among the rest came the friendly dwarf, with the sugarloaf hat, and a new scarlet cloak.

And the wedding was held, and the merry bells run.
And all the good people they danced and they sung,
And feasted and frolick'd I can't tell how long.

Rapunzel

There were once a man and a woman who had long in vain wished for a child. At length the woman hoped that God was about to grant her desire. These people had a little window at the back of their house from which a splendid garden could be seen, which was full of the most beautiful flowers and herbs. It was, however, surrounded by a high wall, and no one dared to go into it because it belonged to an enchantress, who had great power and was dreaded by all the world. One day the woman was standing by this window and looking down into the garden, when she saw a bed which was planted with the most beautiful rampion (rapunzel), and it looked so fresh and green that she longed for it, she quite pined away, and began to look pale and miserable. Then her husband was alarmed, and asked: "What ails you, dear wife?"

"Ah," she replied, "if I can't eat some of the rampion, which is in the garden behind our house, I shall die."

The man, who loved her, thought: "Sooner than let your wife die, bring her some of the rampion yourself, let it cost what it will." At twilight, he clambered down over the wall into the garden of the enchantress, hastily clutched a handful of rampion, and took it to his wife. She at once made herself a salad of it, and ate it greedily. It tasted so good to her—so very good, that the next day she longed for it three times as much as before. If he was to have any rest, her husband must once more descend into the garden. In the gloom of evening therefore, he let himself down again; but when he had clambered down the wall he was terribly afraid, for he saw the enchantress standing before him.

"How can you dare," said she with angry look, "descend into my garden and steal my rampion like a thief? You shall suffer for it!"

"Ah," answered he, "let mercy take the place of justice, I only made up my mind to do it out of necessity. My wife saw your rampion from the window, and felt such a longing for it that she would have died if she had not got some to eat."

Then the enchantress allowed her anger to be softened, and said to him: "If the case be as you say, I will allow you to take away with you as much rampion as you will, only I make one condition, you must give me the child which your wife will bring into the world; it shall be well treated, and I will care for it like a mother." The man in his terror consented to everything, and when the woman was brought to bed, the enchantress appeared at once, gave the child the name of Rapunzel, and took it away with her.

Rapunzel grew into the most beautiful child under the sun. When she was twelve years old, the enchantress shut her into a tower, which lay in a forest, and had neither stairs nor door, but quite at the top was a little window. When the enchantress wanted to go in, she placed herself beneath it and cried:

"RAPUNZEL, RAPUNZEL,
LET DOWN YOUR HAIR TO ME."

Rapunzel had magnificent long hair, fine as spun gold, and when she heard the voice of the enchantress she unfastened her braided tresses, wound them round one of the hooks of the window above, and then the hair fell twenty ells down, and the enchantress climbed up by it.

After a year or two, it came to pass that the king's son rode through the forest and passed by the tower. Then he heard a song, which was so charming that he stood still and listened. This was Rapunzel, who in her solitude passed her time in letting her sweet voice resound. The king's son wanted to climb up to her, and looked for the door of the tower, but none was to be found. He rode home, but the singing had so deeply touched his heart, that every day he went out into the forest and listened to it. Once when he was thus standing behind a tree, he saw that an enchantress came there, and he heard how she cried:

"RAPUNZEL, RAPUNZEL,
LET DOWN YOUR HAIR TO ME."

Then Rapunzel let down the braids of her hair, and the enchantress climbed up to her. "If that is the ladder by which one mounts, I too will try my fortune," said he, and the next day when it began to grow dark, he went to the tower and cried:

"RAPUNZEL, RAPUNZEL,
LET DOWN YOUR HAIR TO ME."

Immediately the hair fell down and the king's son climbed up.

At first Rapunzel was terribly frightened when a man, such as her eyes had never yet beheld, came to her; but the king's son began to talk to her quite like a friend, and told her that his heart had been so stirred that it had let him have no rest, and he had been forced to see her.

Then Rapunzel lost her fear, and when he asked her if she would take him for her husband, and she saw that he was young and handsome, she thought: "He will love me more than old Dame Gothel does"; and she said yes, and laid her hand in his. She said: "I will willingly go away with you, but I do not know how to get down. Bring with you a skein of silk every time that you come, and I will weave a ladder with it, and when that is ready I will descend, and you will take me on your horse." They agreed that until that time he should come to her every evening, for the old woman came by day.

The enchantress remarked nothing of this, until once Rapunzel said to her: "Tell me, Dame Gothel, how it happens that you are so much heavier for me to draw up than the young king's son—he is with me in a moment."

"Ah! you wicked child," cried the enchantress. "What do I hear you say! I thought I had separated you from all the world, and yet you have deceived me!" In her anger she clutched Rapunzel's beautiful tresses, wrapped them twice round her left hand, seized a pair of scissors with the right, and snip, snap, they were cut off, and the lovely braids lay on the ground. And she was so pitiless that she took poor Rapunzel into a desert where she had to live in great grief and misery.

On the same day that she cast out Rapunzel, however, the enchantress fastened the braids of hair, which she had cut off, to the hook of the window, and when the king's son came and cried:

"RAPUNZEL, RAPUNZEL,
LET DOWN YOUR HAIR TO ME."

she let the hair down. The king's son ascended, but instead of finding his dearest Rapunzel, he found the enchantress, who gazed at him with wicked and venomous looks.

"Aha!" she cried mockingly, "you would fetch your dearest, but the beautiful bird sits no longer singing in the nest; the cat has got it, and will scratch out your eyes as well. Rapunzel is lost to you; you will never see her again."

The king's son was beside himself with pain, and in his despair he leapt down from the tower. He escaped with his life, but the thorns into which he fell pierced his eyes. Then he wandered quite blind about the forest, ate nothing but roots and berries, and did naught but lament and weep over the loss of his dearest wife. Thus he roamed about in misery for some years, and at length came to the desert where Rapunzel, with the twins to which she had given birth, a boy and a girl, lived in wretchedness. He heard a voice, and it seemed so familiar to him that he went towards it, and when he approached, Rapunzel knew him and fell on his neck and wept. Two of her tears wetted his eyes and they grew clear again, and he could see with them as before. He led her to his kingdom where he was joyfully received, and they lived for a long time afterwards, happy and contented.

Letters

Alexander Hamilton

1755?-1804

To Elizabeth Schuyler

October 5, 1780

Tappan, New York

I have told you, and I told you truly that I love you too much. You engross my thoughts too intirely to allow me to think of any thing else—you not only employ my mind all day; but you intrude upon my sleep. I meet you in every dream—and when I wake I cannot close my eyes again for ruminating on your sweetness. 'Tis a pretty story indeed that I am to be thus monopolized, by a little *nut-brown maid* like you—and from a statesman and a soldier metamorphosed into a puny lover. I believe in my soul you are an inchantress; but I have tried in vain, if not to break, at least, to weaken the charm—you maintain your empire in spite of all my efforts—and after every new one, I make to withdraw myself from my allegiance my partial heart still returns and clings to you with increased attachment. To drop figure my lovely girl you become dearer to me every moment. I am more and more unhappy and impatient under the hard necessity that keeps me from you, and yet the prospect lengthens as I advance. . . .

I had hoped the middle would have given us to each other; but I now fear it will be the latter end. Though the period of our reunion in reality approaches it seems further off. Among other causes of uneasiness, I dread lest you should imagine, I yield too easily to the barrs that keep us asunder; but if you have such an idea you ought to banish it and reproach yourself with injustice. A spirit entering into bliss, heaven opening upon all its faculties, cannot long more ardently for the enjoyment, than I do my darling Betsey, to taste the heaven that awaits me in your bosom. Is my language too strong? It is a feeble picture of my feelings—no words can tell you how much I love and how much I long—you will only know it when wrapt in each others arms we give and take those delicious caresses which love inspired and marriage sanctifies. . . .

I ought at least to hear from you by every post and your last letter is as old as the middle of Sept. . . . You will laugh at me for consulting you about such a trifle; but I want to know, whether you would prefer my receiving the nuptial benediction in my uniform or in a different habit. It will be just as you please; so consult your whim and what you think most consistent with propriety. If you mean to follow our plan of being secretly married, the scruple ought to appear entirely your own, and you should begin to give hints of it. . . .

I am composing a piece, of which . . . I shall endeavour to prevail upon her to act the principal character. The title is "*the way to get him*, for the benefit of all single ladies who desire to be married." You will ask her, if she has any objection to taking a part in this piece, and tell her that, if am not much mistaken in her, I am sure she will have none. For your own part, your business now is to study "the way to keep him"—which is said to be much the most difficult task of the two; though in your case I verily believe it will be an easy one, and that to succeed effectually you will only have to wish it sincerely. May I only be as successful in pleasing you, and may you be as happy as I shall ever wish to make you.

A Hamilton

To Elizabeth Schuyler

October 13, 1780

Preakness, New Jersey

I would not have you imagine Miss that I write to you so often either to gratify your wishes or to please your vanity; but merely to indulge myself and to comply with that restless propensity of my mind, which will not allow me to be happy when I am not doing something in which you are concerned. This may seem a very idle disposition in a philosopher and a soldier; but I can plead illustrious examples in my justification. Achilles had liked to have sacrificed Greece and his glory to his passion for a female captive; and Anthony lost the world for a woman. I am sorry the times are so changed as to oblige me to summon antiquity for my apology, but I confess, to the disgrace of the present age, that I have not been able to find many who are as far gone as myself in such laudable zeal for the fair sex. I suspect, however, if others knew the charms of my sweetheart as well as I do, I should have a great number of competitors. I wish I could give you an idea of her; you have no conception how sweet a girl she is; it is only in my heart that her image is truly drawn. She has a lovely form, and a mind still more lovely; she is all goodness, the gentlest, the dearest, the tenderest of her sex—ah, Betsey, how I love her!

Two days since I wrote to you my dear girl and sent the letter to the care of Colonel Morris: there was with it a bundle to your mamma, directed to your father, containing a cloak which Miss Livingston sent to my care. I enclosed you in that letter, the copy of a long one to my friend Laurens with an account of Arnold's affair. I mention this for fear of a miscarriage as usual.

Well, my love, here is the middle of October; a few weeks more and you are mine; a sweet reflection to me; is it so to my charmer? Do you find yourself more or less anxious for the moment to arrive as it approaches? This is a good criterion to determine the degree of your affection by. You have had an age for consideration, time enough for even a woman to know her mind in. Do you begin to repent or not? Remember you are going to do a very serious thing. For though our sex have generously given up a part of its prerogatives, and husbands have no longer the power of life and death, as the wiser husbands of former days had, yet we still retain the power of happiness and misery; and if you are prudent you will not trust the felicity of your future life to one in whom you have not good reason for implicit confidence. I give you warning; don't blame me if you make an injudicious choice; and if you should be disposed to retract, don't give me the trouble of a journey to Albany, and then do as did a certain lady I have mentioned to you, find out the day before we are to be married that you "can't like the man"; but of all things I pray you don't make the discovery afterwards, for this would be worse than all. But I do not apprehend its being the case. I think we know each other well enough to understand each other's feelings, and to be sure our affection will not only last but be progressive.

I stopped to read over my letter; it is a motley mixture of fond extravagance and sprightly dullness; the truth is I am too much in love to be either reasonable or witty; I feel in the extreme; and when I attempt to speak of my feelings I rave. I have remarked to you before that real tenderness has always a tincture of sadness, and when I affect the lively my melting heart rebels. It is separated from you and it cannot be cheerful. Love is a sort of insanity and every thing I write savors strongly of it; that you return it is the best proof of your madness also.

TO ELIZABETH SCHUYLER

I tell you, my Betsey, you are negligent; you do not write me often enough. Take more care of my happiness, for there is nothing your Hamilton would not do to promote yours.

John Keats

1795–1821

To Fanny Brawne

July 3, 1819

Newport

My dearest Lady,

I am glad I had not an opportunity of sending off a Letter which I wrote for you on Tuesday night—'twas too much like one out of Rousseau's Heloise. I am more reasonable this morning. The morning is the only proper time for me to write to a beautiful Girl whom I love so much: for at night, when the lonely day has closed, and the lonely, silent, unmusical Chamber is waiting to receive me as into a Sepulchre, then believe me my passion gets entirely the sway, then I would not have you see those Rhapsodies which I once thought it impossible I should ever give way to, and which I have often laughed at in another, for fear you should [think me] either too unhappy or perhaps a little mad.

I am now at a very pleasant Cottage window, looking onto a beautiful hilly country, with a glimpse of the sea; the morning is very fine. I do not know how elastic my spirit might be, what pleasure I might have in living here and breathing and wandering as free as a stag about this beautiful Coast if the remembrance of you did not weigh so upon me I have never known any unalloy'd Happiness for many days together: the dearth or sickness of some one has always spoilt my hours, and now when none such troubles oppress me, it is you must confess very hard that another sort of pain should haunt me.

Ask yourself my love whether you are not very cruel to have so entrammelled me, so destroyed my freedom. Will you confess this in the Letter you must write immediately, and do all you can to console me in it, make it rich as a draught of poppies to intoxicate me, write the softest words and kiss them that I may at least touch my lips where yours have been. For myself I know not how to express my devotion to so fair a form: I want a brighter word than bright, a fairer word than fair. I almost wish we were butterflies and liv'd but three summer days—three such days with you I could fill with more delight than fifty common years could ever contain. But however selfish I may feel, I am sure I could never act selfishly: as I told you a day or two before I left Hampstead, I will never return to London if my Fate does not turn up Pam or at least a Court-card. Though I could centre my Happiness in you, I cannot expect to engross your heart so entirely, indeed if I thought you felt as much for me as I do for you at this moment I do not think I could restrain myself from seeing you again tomorrow for the delight of one embrace.

But no, I must live upon hope and Chance. In case of the worst that can happen, I shall still love you, but what hatred shall I have for another!

Some lines I read the other day are continually ringing a peal in my ears:

To see those eyes I prize above mine own
    Dart favors on another—
And those sweet lips (yielding immortal nectar)
    Be gently press'd by any but myself—
Think, think Francesca, what a cursed thing
    It were beyond expression!

J.

Do write immediately. There is no Post from this Place, so you must address Post Office, Newport, Isle of Wight. I know before night I shall curse myself for having sent you so cold a Letter; yet it is better to do it as much in my senses as possible. Be as kind as the distance will permit to your

J. Keats.

Present my Compliments to your mother, my love to Margaret and best remembrances to your Brother, if you please so.

To Fanny Brawne

March 1820

Sweetest Fanny,

You fear, sometimes, I do not love you so much as you wish? My dear Girl I love you ever and ever and without reserve. The more I have known you the more have I lov'd. In every way—even my jealousies have been agonies of Love, in the hottest fit I ever had I would have died for you. I have vex'd you too much. But for Love! Can I help it? You are always new. The last of your kisses was ever the sweetest; the last smile the brightest; the last movement the gracefullest. When you pass'd my window home yesterday, I was fill'd with as much admiration as if I had then seen you for the first time. You uttered a half complaint once that I only lov'd your Beauty. Have I nothing else then to love in you but that? Do not I see a heart naturally furnish'd with wings imprison itself with me? No ill prospect has been able to turn your thoughts a moment from me. This perhaps should be as much a subject of sorrow as joy—but I will not talk of that. Even if you did not love me I could not help an entire devotion to you: how much more deeply then must I feel for you knowing you love me. My Mind has been the most discontented and restless one that ever was put into a body too small for it. I never felt my Mind repose upon anything with complete and undistracted enjoyment—upon no person but you. When you are in the room my thoughts never fly out of window: you always concentrate my whole senses. The anxiety shown about our Love in your last note is an immense pleasure to me; however you must not suffer such speculations to molest you any more: not will I any more believe you can have the least pique against me. Brown is gone out—but here is Mrs. Wylie—when she is gone I shall be awake for you.—Remembrances to your Mother.

Your affectionate,
J. Keats.

To Fanny Brawne

May 1820

My dearest Girl,

I wrote a Letter for you yesterday expecting to have seen your mother. I shall be selfish enough to send it though I know it may give you a little pain, because I wish you to see how unhappy I am for love of you, and endeavour as much as I can to entice you to give up your whole heart to me whose whole existence hangs upon you. You could not step or move an eyelid but it would shoot to my heart—I am greedy of you—Do not think of any thing but me. Do not live as if I was not existing—Do not forget me—But have I any right to say you forget me? Perhaps you think of me all day. Have I any right to wish you to be unhappy for me? You would forgive me for wishing it, if you knew the extreme passion I have that you should love me—and for you to love me as I do you, you must think of no one but me, much less write that sentence. Yesterday and this morning.

I have been haunted with a sweet vision—I have seen you the whole time in your shepherdess dress. How my senses have ached at it! How my heart has been devoted to it! How my eyes have been full of Tears at it! I[n]deed I think a real Love is enough to occupy the widest heart—Your going to town alone, when I heard of it was a shock to me— yet I expected it—promise me you will not for some time, till I get better. Promise me this and fill the paper full of the most endearing names. If you cannot do so with good will, do my Love tell me—say what you think—confess if your heart is too much fasten'd on the world. Perhaps then I may see you at a greater distance, I may not be able to appropriate you so closely to myself. Were you to loose a favorite bird from the cage, how would your eyes ache after it as long as it was in sight; when out of sight you would recover a little. Perhaps if you would, if so it is, confess to me how many things are necessary to you besides me, I might be happier, by being less tantaliz'd. Well may you exclaim, how selfish, how cruel, not to let me enjoy my youth! to wish me to be unhappy! You must be so if you love me—upon my Soul I can be contented with nothing else. If you could really what is call'd enjoy yourself at a Party—if you can smile in peoples faces, and wish them to admire you now, you never have nor ever will love me—I see life in nothing but the cerrtainty of your Love—convince me of it my sweetest. If I am not somehow convinc'd I shall die of agony. If we love we must not live as other men and women do—I cannot brook the wolfsbane of fashion and foppery and tattle. You must be mine to die upon the rack if I want you. I do not pretend to say I have more feeling than my fellows—but I wish you seriously to look over my letters kind and unkind and consider whether the Person who wrote them can be able to endure much longer the agonies and uncertainties which you are so peculiarly made to create—My recovery of bodily health will be of no benefit to me if you are not all mine when I am well. For god's sake save me—or tell me my passion is of too awful a nature for you. Again God bless you

J.K.

No, my sweet Fanny, I am wrong. I do not want you to be unhappy, and yet I do, I must while there is so sweet a Beauty—my loveliest my darling! Good bye! I kiss you—O the torments!

Robert Browning

1812–1889

To Elizabeth Barrett

September 13, 1845

Now, dearest, I will try and write the little I shall be able, in reply to your letter of last week— and first of all I have to entreat you, now more than ever, to help me and understand from the few words the feelings behind them—(should *speak* rather more easily, I think—but I dare not run the risk: and I know, after all, you will be just and kind where you can). I have read your letter again and again. I will tell you—no, not *you*, but any imaginary other person, who should hear what

I am going to avow; I would tell that person most sincerely there is not a particle of fatuity, shall I call it, in that avowal; cannot be, seeing that from the beginning and at this moment I never dreamed of winning your *love*. I can hardly write this word, so incongruous and impossible does it seem; such a change of our places does it imply—nor, next to that, though long after, *would* I, if I *could*, supplant one of any of the affections that I know to have taken root in you—*that* great and solemn one, for instance. I feel that if I could get myself *remade*, as if turned to gold, I would not even then desire to become more than the mere setting to *that* diamond you must always wear. The regard and esteem you now give me, in this letter, and which I press to my heart and bow my head upon, is all I can take and all too embarrassing, using *all* my gratitude. And yet, with that contented pride in being infinitely your debtor as it is, bound to you for ever as it is; when I read your letter with all the determination to be just to us both; I dare not so far withstand the light I am master of, as to refuse seeing that whatever is recorded as an objection to your disposing of that life of mine I would give you, has reference to some supposed good in that life which your accepting it would destroy (of which fancy I shall speak presently)—I say, wonder as I may at this, I cannot but find it there, surely there. I could no more 'bind *you* by words,' than you have bound me, as you say—but if I misunderstand you, one assurance to that effect will be but too intelligible to me—but, as it *is*, I have difficulty in imagining that while one of so many reasons, which I am not obliged to repeat to myself, but which any one easily conceives; while *any one* of those reasons would impose silence on me *for ever* (for, as I observed, I love you as you now are, and *would* not remove one affection that is already part of you,)—*would* you, being able to speak *so*, only say *that you* desire not to put 'more sadness than I was born to,' into my life?—that you 'could give me only what it were ungenerous to give'?

Have I your meaning here? In so many words, is it on my account that you bid me 'leave this subject'? I think if it were so, I would for once call my advantages round me. I am not what your generous self-forgetting appreciation would sometimes make me out—but it is not since yesterday, nor ten nor twenty years before, that I began to look into my own life, and study its end, and requirements, what would turn to its good or its loss—and I *know*, if one may know anything, that to make that life yours and increase it by union with yours, would render me *supremely happy*, as I said, and say, and feel. My whole suit to you is, in that sense, *selfish*— not that I am ignorant that *your* nature would most surely attain happiness in being conscious that it made another happy—but *that best, best end of all*, would, like the rest, come from yourself, be a reflection of your own gift.

Dearest, I will end here—words, persuasion, arguments, if they were at my service I would not use them—I believe in you, altogether have faith in you—in you. I will not think of insulting by trying to reassure you on one point which certain phrases in your letter might at first glance seem to imply—you do not understand me to be living and labouring and writing (and *not* writing) in order to be successful in the world's sense? I even convinced the people *here* what was my true 'honourable position in society,' &c. &c. therefore I shall not have to inform *you* that I desire to be very rich, very great; but not in reading Law gratis with dear foolish old Basil Montagu, as he ever and anon bothers me to do;—much less—enough of this nonsense.

'Tell me what I have a claim to hear': I can hear it, and be as grateful as I was before and am now—your friendship is my pride and happiness. If you told me your love was bestowed elsewhere, and that it was in my power to serve you *there*, to serve you there would still be my pride and happiness. I look on and on over the prospect of my love, it is all *on*wards—and all possible forms of unkindness . . . I quite laugh to think how they are *behind* . . . cannot be encountered in the route we are travelling! I submit to you and will obey you implicitly—obey what I am able to conceive of your least desire, much more of your expressed wish. But it was necessary to make this avowal, among other reasons, for one which the world would recognize too. My whole scheme of life (with its wants, material wants at least, closely cut down) was long ago calculated—and it supposed *you*, the finding such an one as you, utterly impossible— because in calculating one goes upon *chances*, not on providence—how could I expect you? So for my own future way in the world I have always refused to care—any one who can live a couple of years and more on bread and potatoes as I did once on a time, and who prefers a blouse and a blue shirt (such as I now write in) to all manner of dress and gentlemanly appointment, and who can, if necessary, groom a horse not so badly, or at all events would rather do it all day long than succeed Mr. Fitzroy Kelly in the Solicitor-Generalship,—such an one need not very much concern himself beyond considering the lilies how they grow. But now I see you near this life, all changes—and at a word, I will do all that ought to be done, that every one used to say could be done, and let 'all my powers find sweet employ' as

Dr. Watts sings, in getting whatever is to be got—not very much, surely. I would print these things, get them away, and do this now, and go to you at Pisa with the news—at Pisa where one may live for some £100 a year—while, lo, I seem to remember, I *do* remember, that Charles Kean offered to give me 500 of those pounds for any play that might suit him—to say nothing of Mr. Colburn saying confidentially that he wanted more than his dinner 'a novel on the subject of *Napoleon*'! So may one make money, if one does not live in a house in a row, and feel impelled to take the Princess's Theatre for a laudable development and exhibition of one's faculty.

Take the sense of all this, I beseech you, dearest—all you shall say will be best—I am yours—

Yes, Yours ever. God bless you for all you have been, and are, and will certainly be to me, come what He shall please!

R.B.

To Elizabeth Barrett

November 17, 1845

At last your letter comes—and the deep joy—(I know and use to analyse my own feelings, and be sober in giving distinctive names to their varieties; this is *deep* joy,)—the true love with which I take this much of you into my heart, . . . *that* proves what it is I wanted so long, and find at last, and am happy for ever. I must have more than 'intimated'—I must have spoken plainly out the truth, if I do myself the barest justice, and told you long ago that the admiration at your works went *away*, quite another way and afar from the love of you. If I could fancy some method of what I shall say happening without all the obvious stumbling-blocks of falseness, &c. which no foolish fancy dares associate with you . . . if you could tell me when I next sit by you—'I will undeceive you,—I am not *the* Miss B.—she is up-stairs and you shall see her—I only wrote those letters, and am what you see, that is all now left you' (all the misapprehension having arisen from *me*, in some inexplicable way) . . . I should not begin by *saying* anything, dear, dearest—but *after that*, I should assure you—soon make you believe that I did not much wonder at the event, for I have been all my life asking what connection there is between the satisfaction at the display of power, and the sympathy with—ever-increasing sympathy with—all imaginable weakness? Look now: Coleridge writes on and on,—at last he writes a note to his 'War-Eclogue,' in which he avers himself to have been actuated by a really—on the whole—*benevolent* feeling to Mr. Pitt when he wrote that stanza in which 'Fire' means to 'cling to him everlastingly'—where is the long line of admiration now that the end snaps? And now—here I refuse to fancy—you know whether, if you never write another line, speak another intelligible word, recognize me by a look again—whether I shall love you less or *more* . . . more; having a right to expect more strength with the strange emergency. And it is because I know this, build upon this entirely, that as a reasonable creature, I am bound to look first to what hangs farthest and most loosely from me . . . what *might* go from you to your loss, and so to mine, to say the least . . . because I want all of you, not just so much as I could not live without—and because I see the danger of your entirely generous disposition and cannot quite, yet, bring myself to profit by it in the quiet way you recommend. Always remember, I never wrote to you, all the years, on the strength of your poetry, though I constantly heard of you through Mr. K. and was near seeing you once, and

might have easily availed myself of his interven-
tion to commend any letter to your notice, so as
to reach you out of the foolish crowd of rushers-in
upon genius . . . who come and eat their bread
and cheese on the high-altar, and talk of reverence
without one of its surest instincts—never quiet till
they cut their initials on the cheek of the Medicean
Venus to prove they worship her. My admiration,
as I said, went its natural way in silence—but
when on my return to England in December, late
in the month, Mr. K. sent those Poems to my sister, and I read my name there—and when, a day
or two after, I met him and, beginning to speak
my mind on them, and getting on no better than
I should now, said quite naturally—'if I were to
write this, now?'—and he assured me with his perfect kindness, you would be even 'pleased' to hear
from me under those circumstances . . . nay,—for
I will tell you all, in this, in everything—when he
wrote me a note soon after to reassure me on that
point . . . then I *did* write, on *account of my purely
personal obligation*, though of course taking that

occasion to allude to the general and customary delight in your works: I did write, on the whole, unwillingly . . . with consciousness of having to *speak* on a subject which I *felt* thoroughly concerning, and could not be satisfied with an imperfect expression of. As for expecting then what has followed . . . I shall only say I was scheming how to get done with England and go to my heart in Italy. And now, my love—I am round you . . . my whole life is wound up and down and over you. . . . I feel you stir everywhere. I am not conscious of thinking or feeling but *about* you, with some reference to you—so I will live, so may I die! And you have blessed me *beyond* the *bond*, in more than in giving me yourself to love; inasmuch as you believed me from the first . . . what you call 'dream-work' *was* real of its kind, did you not think? and now you believe me, *I* believe and am happy, in what I write with my heart full of love for you. Why do you tell me of a doubt, as now, and bid me not clear it up, 'not answer you'? Have I done wrong in thus answering? Never, never do *me* direct *wrong* and hide for a moment from me what a word can explain as now. You see, you thought, if but for a moment, I loved your intellect—or what predominates in your poetry and is most distinct from your heart—better, or as well as you—did you not? and I have told you every thing,—explained everything . . . have I not? And now I will dare . . . yes, dearest, kiss you back to my heart again; my own. There—and there!

And since I wrote what is above, I have been reading among other poems that sonnet—'Past and Future'—which affects me more than any poem I ever read. How can I put your poetry away from you, even in these ineffectual attempts to concentrate myself upon, and better apply myself to what remains?—poor, poor work it is; for is not that sonnet to be loved as a true utterance of yours? I cannot attempt to put down the thoughts that rise; may God bless me, as you pray, by letting that beloved hand shake the less . . . I will only ask, *the less* . . . for being laid on mine through this life! And, indeed, you write down, for me to calmly read, that I make you happy! Then it is—as with all power—God through the weakest instrumentality . . . and I am past expression proud and grateful—My love,

I am your
R.B.

I must answer your questions: I am better—and will certainly have your injunction before my eyes and work quite moderately. Your letters come *straight* to me—my father's go to Town, except on extraordinary occasions, so that *all* come for my first looking-over. I saw Mr. K. last night at the Amateur Comedy—and heaps of old acquaintances—and came home tired and savage—and *yearned* literally, for a letter this morning, and so it came and I was well again. So, I am not even to have your low spirits leaning on mine? It was just because I always find you alike, and *ever* like yourself, that I seemed to discern a depth, when you spoke of 'some days' and what they made uneven where all is agreeable to *me*. Do not, now, deprive me of a right—a right . . . to find you as you *are*; get no habit of being cheerful with me—I have universal sympathy and can show you a side of me, a true face, turn as you may. If you *are* cheerful . . . so will I be . . . if sad, my cheerfulness will be all the while *behind*, and propping up, any sadness that meets yours, if that should be necessary. As for my question about the opium . . . you do not misunderstand *that* neither: I trust in the eventual consummation of my—shall I not say, *our*—hopes; and all that bears upon your health immediately or prospectively, affects me— how it affects me! Will you write again? *Wednesday*, remember! Mr. K. wants me to go to him one of the three next days after. I will bring you some let- ters . . . one from Landor. Why should I trouble you about 'Pomfret.'

And Luria . . . does it so interest you? Better is to come of it. How you lift me up!—

Elizabeth Barrett Browning

1806–1861

To Robert Browning

December 20, 1845

Dearest, you know how to say what makes me happiest, you who never think, you say, of making me happy! For my part I do not think of it either; I simply understand that you *are* my happiness, and that therefore you could not make another happiness for me, such as would be worth having—not even *you*! Why, how could you? *That* was in my mind to speak yesterday, but I could not speak it— to write it, is easier.

Talking of happiness—shall I tell you? Promise not to be angry and I will tell you. I have thought sometimes that, if I considered myself wholly, I should choose to die this winter—now—before I had disappointed you in anything. But because you are better and dearer and more to be considered than I, I do *not* choose it. I *cannot* choose to give you any pain, even on the chance of its being a less pain, a less evil, than what may follow perhaps (who can say?), if I should prove the burden of your life.

For if you make me happy with some words, you frighten me with others—as with the extravagance yesterday—and seriously—*too* seriously, when the moment for smiling at them is past—I am frightened, I tremble! When you come to know me as well as I know myself, what can save me, do you think, from disappointing and displeasing you? I ask the question, and find no answer.

It is a poor answer, to say that I can do one thing well . . . that I have one capacity largely. On points of the general affections, I have in thought applied to myself the words of Mme. de Stael, not fretfully, I hope, not complainingly, I am sure (I can thank God for most affectionate friends!) not complainingly, yet mournfully and in profound conviction—those words—'*jamais je n'ai pas été aimée comme j'aime.*' The capacity of loving is the largest of my powers I think—I thought so before knowing you—and one form of feeling. And although any woman might love you—*every* woman,—with understanding enough to discern you by—(oh, do not fancy that I am unduly magnifying mine office) yet I persist in persuading myself that! Because I have the capacity, as I said—and besides I owe more to you than others could, it seems to me: let me boast of it. To many, you might be better than all things while one of all things: to me you are instead of all—to many, a crowning happiness—to me, the happiness itself. From out of the deep dark pits men see the stars more gloriously—and *de profundis amavi*—

It is a very poor answer! Almost as poor an answer as yours could be if I were to ask you to teach me to please you always; or rather, how not to

287

displease you, disappoint you, vex you—what if all those things were in my fate?

And—(to begin!)—*I* am disappointed to-night. I expected a letter which does not come—and I had felt so sure of having a letter to-night . . . unreasonably sure perhaps, which means doubly sure.

Friday.—Remember you have had two notes of mine, and that it is certainly not my turn to write, though I am writing.

Scarcely you had gone on Wednesday when Mr. Kenyon came. It seemed best to me, you know, that you should go—I had the presentiment of his footsteps—and so near they were, that if you had looked up the street in leaving the door, you must have seen him! Of course I told him of your having been here and also at his house; whereupon he enquired eagerly if you meant to dine with him, seeming disappointed by my negative. 'Now I had told him,' he said . . . and murmured on to himself loud enough for me to hear, that 'it would have been a peculiar pleasure &c.' The reason I have not seen him lately is the eternal 'business,' just as you thought, and he means to come 'oftener now,' so nothing is wrong as I half thought.

As your letter does not come it is a good opportunity for asking what sort of ill humour, or (to be more correct) bad temper, you most particularly admire—sulkiness?—the divine gift of sitting aloof in a cloud like any god for three weeks together perhaps—pettishness? . . . which will get you up a storm about a crooked pin or a straight one either? obstinacy?—which is an agreeable form of temper I can assure you, and describes itself—or the good open passion which lies on the floor and kicks, like one of my cousins?—Certainly I prefer the last, and should, I think, prefer it (as an evil), even if it were not the born weakness of my own nature—though I humbly confess (to *you*, who seem to think differently of these things) that never since I was a child have I upset all the chairs and tables and thrown the books about the room in a fury—I am afraid I do not even 'kick,' like my cousin, now. Those demonstrations were all done by the 'light of other days'—not a very full light, I used to be accustomed to think:—but *you*,—*you* think otherwise, *you* take a fury to be the opposite of 'indifference,' as if there could be no such thing as self-control! Now for my part, I do believe that the worst-tempered persons in the world are less so through sensibility than selfishness—they spare nobody's heart, on the ground of being themselves pricked by a straw. Now see if it isn't so. What, after all, is a good temper but generosity in trifles—and what, without it, is the happiness of life? We have only to look round us. I *saw* a woman, once, burst into tears, because her husband cut the bread and butter too thick. I saw *that* with my own eyes. Was it *sensibility*, I wonder! They were at least real tears and ran down her cheeks. 'You *always* do it'! she said.

Why how you must sympathize with the heroes and heroines of the French romances (*do* you sympathize with them very much?) when at the slightest provocation they break up the tables and chairs, (a degree beyond the deeds of my childhood!—*I* only used to upset them) break up the tables and chairs and chiffoniers, and dash the china to atoms. The

men *do* the furniture, and the women the porcelain:
and pray observe that they always set about this as
a matter of course! When they have broken everything in the room, they sink down quite (and very
naturally) *abattus*. I remember a particular case of
a hero of Frederic Soulié's, who, in the course of an
'emotion,' takes up a chair *unconsciously*, and breaks
it into very small pieces, and then proceeds with his
soliloquy. Well!—the clearest idea this excites in *me*,
is of the low condition in Paris, of moral govern-
ment and of upholstery. Because—just consider
for yourself—how *you* would succeed in breaking
to pieces even a three-legged stool if it were prop-
erly put together—as stools are in England—just
yourself, without a hammer and a screw! You might
work at it *comme quatre*, and find it hard to finish, I
imagine. And then as a demonstration, a child of six
years old might demonstrate just so (in his sphere)
and be whipped accordingly.

How I go on writing!—and you, who do not
write at all!—two extremes, one set against the
other.

But I must say, though in ever such an ill temper (which you know is just the time to select for writing a panegyric upon good temper) that I am glad you do not despise my own right name too much, because I never was called Elizabeth by any one who loved me at all, and I accept the omen. So little it seems my name that if a voice said suddenly 'Elizabeth,' I should as soon turn round as my sisters would . . . no sooner. Only, my own right name has been complained of for want of euphony . . . *Ba* . . . now and then it has—and Mr. Boyd makes a compromise and calls me *Elibet*, because nothing could induce him to desecrate his organs accustomed to Attic harmonics, with a *Ba*. So I am glad, and accept the omen.

But I give you no credit for not thinking that I may forget you . . . I! As if you did not see the difference! Why, *I* could not even forget to *write* to *you*, observe!—

Whenever you write, say how you are. Were you wet on Wednesday?

Your own—

To Robert Browning

March 7, 1846

Always *you*, is it, who torments me? always *you*? Well! I agree to bear the torments as Socrates his persecution by the potters:—and by the way he liked those potters, as Plato shows, and was fain to go to them for his illustrations . . . as I to you for all my light. Also, while we are on the subject, I will tell you another fault of your Bartoli . . . his 'choice Tuscan' filled one of my pages, in the place of my English better than Tuscan.

For the letter you mentioned, I meant to have said in mine yesterday, that I was grateful to you for telling me of it—*that* was one of the prodigalities of your goodness to me . . . not thrown away, in one sense, however superfluous. Do you ever think how I must feel when you overcome me with all this generous tenderness, only beloved! I cannot say it.

Because it is colder to-day I have not been down-stairs but let to-morrow be warm enough—*facilis descensus*. There's something infernal to me really, in the going down, and now too that our cousin is here! Think of his beginning to attack Henrietta the other day. . . . '*So* Mr. C. has retired and left the field to Surtees Cook. Oh . . . you needn't deny . . . it's the news of all the world except your father. And as to *him*, I don't blame you—he never will consent to the marriage of son or daughter. Only you should consider, you know, because he won't leave you a shilling, &c. &c. . . .' You hear the sort of man. And then in a minute after . . . 'And what is this about Ba?' 'About Ba' said my sisters, 'why who has been persuading you of such nonsense?' 'Oh, my authority is very good,—perfectly unnecessary for you to tell any stories, Arabel,—a literary friendship, is it?' . . . and so on . . . after that fashion! This comes from my brothers of course, but we need not be afraid of its passing *beyond*, I think, though I was a good deal vexed when I heard first of it last night and have been in cousinly anxiety ever since to get our Orestes safe away from those Furies his creditors, into Brittany again. He is an intimate friend of my brothers besides the relationship, and they talk to him as to each other, only they oughtn't to have talked *that*, and without knowledge too.

I forgot to tell you that Mr. Kenyon was in an immoderate joy the day I saw him last, about Mr. Poe's 'Raven' as seen in the *Athenæum* extracts, and came to ask what I knew of the poet and his poetry, and took away the book. It's the rhythm which has taken him with 'glamour' I fancy. Now you will stay on Monday till the last moment, and go to him for dinner at six.

Who 'looked in at the door?' Nobody. But Arabel a little way opened it, and hearing your voice, went back. There was no harm—*is* no fear of harm. Nobody in the house would find his or her pleasure in running the risk of giving me pain. I mean my brothers and sisters would not.

Are you trying the music to charm the brain to stillness? Tell me. And keep from that 'Soul's Tragedy' which did so much harm—oh, that I had bound you by some Stygian oath not to touch it.

So my rock . . . may the birds drop into your crevices the seeds of all the flowers of the world— only it is not for *those*, that I cling to you as the single rock in the salt sea.

Ever I am
Your own.